The Vampire and the Case of the Perilous Poltergeist

Heather G. Harris & Jilleen Dolbeare

Published by Hellhound Press Limited

Copyright © 2024 by Heather G. Harris and Jilleen Dolbeare

All rights reserved.

No portion of this book may be reproduced in any form without written permission from the publisher or author, except as permitted by U.S. copyright law.

Published by Hellhound Press.

Cover Design by Christian Bentulan.

Heather's Dedication

Thanks to Jill, for continuing to be an absolute inspiration. She is awe-inspiring, and I am so proud and lucky to write books with her.

Jill's Dedication

I dedicate this book to the Alaska State Trooper Academy. They greeted me with open arms, took me on the best tour, answered my multitude of questions, and even let me play with the guns. Extra thanks to Sgt. Boyd Branch, Academy Deputy Commander, for the lovely tour! Sorry for a few changes to things, but we had to sneak in the supernatural!

I dedicate this to my family for standing behind me, and to my fans who support me! Also, thanks to my wonderful writer friends, go FAKAs!

Chapter 1

Thorsen hit the mat with so much force that I heard the air leaving his lungs. Before Sidnee could complete the exercise and cuff him, he rolled away and staggered to his feet.

I met her gaze and deliberately widened my eyes. She was pulling her punches too much; she could easily have subdued him. We were supposed to be hiding that we were supernat, but nobody had said anything about being *incompetent.*

Sidnee grimaced and gave me a fraction of a nod, but before she could rectify her error the instructor pulled her aside. His expression was patient as he explained once again that she was supposed to *cuff* the suspect when he was down.

I wondered whether Sidnee was simply toying with the other recruit as a way to get in as many throws as she could under the guise of ineptitude. Theodore Thorsen was an unmitigated asshole. Young, blond and muscular, he wasn't bad looking – if you didn't look too closely at his soul – but his ego was bigger than his admittedly impressive biceps.

Since Day One at the academy, Thorsen had seemed to have Sidnee and me in his sights. I wasn't sure what his problem was, apart from the fact that we had the audacity to be women, but he didn't seem to have the same issue with any of the other females on the course.

Early in the program Thorsen had made a massive effort to mix and mingle with everyone, but Sidnee and me had been the obvious exceptions; he'd treated us like pariahs. Whilst the others had received well-meaning advice, a helping hand and friendly smiles from him, Sidnee and I got hard glowers.

In the beginning he'd kept them off his face in front of the other recruits and the instructors, but as time passed it was like he'd given up on the mask of civility. We had stopped trying to play nice too, and by this point in our training the gloves were well and truly off on both sides.

Thorsen's face was flushed with anger as his friends teased him for being thrown by a five-foot-two dot of a woman. He was the human equivalent of a Russian doll – totally full of himself – and being beaten like this was eating him alive. Thanks to his overwhelming ignorance of what we were, he had no idea that we had more up our sleeves than sinew and muscle.

When Sidnee looked my way again, I gave her a wide grin and a thumbs up. *Knock him dead!* She nodded then focused as the instructor called for the two of them to engage again.

They circled more cautiously this time – at least on Thorsen's part. Previously he'd tried to blast right at her, thinking he could overpower her with his sheer size and his big-dick energy. Now he knew better and he didn't like it one bit. Men like him wrapped their ignorance around themselves like a cocooning glove; if someone ever told him that he wasn't God's gift, he'd probably faint.

I watched closely. Had he learned his lesson? I doubted it. The irritating thing was that if he actually used his brains rather than his brawn, he could probably take Sid down because she was still second-guessing herself too much. Her uncertainty was clear in her eyes: she was battling imposter syndrome big time. If Thorsen was smart – which at times he *did* seem to be – he could use that hesitation against her.

I watched his jaw clench and his fist bunch. Fuck, he was actually going to go at her with a closed fist, which was totally against the rules. How the hot-headed fool was still on the course, I had no idea.

The tension in the room rocketed; clearly I wasn't the only one who'd spotted the fist. I looked around to see if the instructor, Sergeant Blake, would intervene but he was talking to one of the other recruits and his back was turned to the bout he'd started. Real smart.

My floppy heart gave a beat. Even with Sidnee's supernat strength and healing, if Thorsen hit her with a closed fist he'd send her flying and possibly knock her out for real: physics could be a real bitch. I wanted to yell out a warning her, but I didn't want to break her concentration and make the whole situation ten times worse.

My fists clenched. Should I intercede? Whilst it was my turn to hesitate, Sidnee spotted the fist coming at her and jumped back at the last second so that Thorsen swung wide, and his hand whistled through the air instead. Sidnee's eyes went black as rage swamped her.

Oh shit – she was on the verge of shifting and that was a major no-no! I looked around for a water source and yep, every single recruit had a water bottle with them. Of course they did. There was more than enough water to call to Sidnee's mer instincts, instincts that were telling her to hulk-smash.

'Take a deep breath,' I yelled and her black gaze flicked to me. I pantomimed deep breathing and gave a sigh of relief as she copied me. Her eyes leeched from black to her usual warm brown. Thank fuck for that.

Naturally Thorsen took advantage of her calming exercises to try and hit her again, but now she was focused on him. There wasn't a hint of her sunny nature on her face; she was on it. I relaxed and let a smile curve my lips as I watched the show.

Sidnee danced around Thorsen for a minute or two. He was obviously mortified that she was still on her feet – his face was as red as a Brit's after a week abroad in Ibiza. His hair had flopped over his forehead, where it clung to the sweat beading there. Sexy. By contrast, Sidnee still looked fresh; with her long dark hair tied back in a low ponytail, she was as cool as a sea cucumber.

Her jaw set as she feinted towards him, acting as if she was going to sweep his leg out from under him and take him down. He hastily countered by throwing out an arm to knock her back, but she dodged and jogged back before he could strike her.

As she grinned at him, you could almost see the steam coming from his ears. Instead of pausing and thinking, he charged her again, straight and fast like a raging bull but without the huge swinging bollocks. Like last time, Sidnee grabbed his extended arm; using his momentum against him, she twisted her hips to send him tumbling to the mat. This time she flipped him onto his washboard abs and cuffed him in seconds. To my trained eye she'd used a little of her supernat strength, but only a smidge so that it looked like a standard takedown. Smart.

I clapped loudly and most of the other recruits joined in. Only Thorsen was silent as he all but ate the mat and frothed at his own incompetence.

Sergeant Blake came over, uncuffed him and helped him to his feet. Blake was tall and lithe, in his early forties, and he always radiated an air of calm competence. I liked him a lot; he knew the value of positive reinforcement, unlike another of the instructors, Wilson, who would rather be pissed on than give a word of praise.

'Great work, Fletcher,' Blake said to Sidnee. She preened a little under his approving gaze – she was *such* a teacher's pet – but I couldn't throw stones because I was the same. After years of being starved of positive reinforcement from my parents, praise from the teachers gave me nearly as much of a thrill as an orgasm. Yes, I had issues.

Blake spent a few minutes running through what Thorsen had done wrong, including highlighting the danger we'd get into if we bowed to our emotions in the field. Thorsen's scowl deepened: nice guy, well-rounded, clearly open to criticism.

The sergeant ended the lecture with his personal motto, 'Keep a level head,' and we all groaned a little. We'd heard the phrase roughly sixty-billion times since we'd been at the academy. Apparently keeping your cool was important. Well, who knew? Obviously not Theodore Thorsen.

Blake's other tried-and-trusted phrase was, 'Trust your gut.' Now that I already knew how to do.

Once class was over, Thorsen made a point of barging into my shoulder. He had the maturity of a tempestuous goat; he would headbutt you then act like *you* were the problem. He glared at me. 'You and your little friend better watch yourself, you rodent bitch,' he sneered under his breath.

That was a first; I'd been called all kinds of bunny-adjacent names but this was my first 'rodent'. Maybe he did have two brain cells to rub together after all.

I flashed him a grin and batted my eyelashes. 'Why don't you say that louder? Are you afraid the little girl who handed you your arse might hear you?'

He couldn't do anything to me, and he knew it. The academy would throw you out on your ear for lying, cheating, stealing or abusing another recruit. Thorsen had been pushing almost all those boundaries since we'd arrived nine weeks earlier though he hadn't crossed the line – yet.

He'd flirted pretty hard with Margilene the first week. She'd reported him when he hadn't seemed inclined to listen to her polite instruction to 'buzz off', and he'd been warned about curtailing his unwanted advances. He didn't need to add violence against another recruit to his already blemished record and I didn't want to blemish mine, so I took the high road, ignored him and walked out.

We had fifteen minutes before we had to be back in the classroom and I wanted to text Connor. Thinking of my beau helped scrub the incident from my brain; Thorsen had to be in my physical presence sometimes, but he didn't get any real estate in my mind.

Since we had a break, Sidnee and I hurried to the dorm room we shared with Margi. It was no coincidence that she was also a supernat, a witch. Margi was from the Deep South but she'd moved up from the lower forty-eight for a man. Once she was in Alaska the man had dumped her. What an asshat.

Other than Sidnee, Margi and me, there were only three other women in the academy and no female instructors. The other three women were all ped and slept in the next dorm over from us. The supernat men had also been segregated into one dorm on the other side of the break room. Separating the peds and supernats made it much easier for us to sneak out for our secret extra lessons that were focused on all things supernatural.

Each dorm was set up for four people but having only three of us in the small space was much nicer. The bathrooms were only designed for two – two sinks, two showers, two toilets – so someone always had to wait. Sometimes we only had fifteen minutes each to shower. Homesickness was already wracking me and I dreamed of a twenty-minute shower or maybe even a bath! Heaven.

I didn't want to waste my break today in the bathroom; I needed contact with the outside world more than I needed to be clean. instead, I threw myself on my bed and reached into my footlocker for my phone.

There were three text messages waiting for me. Crap: what was wrong now?

Chapter 2

My gut clenched because the first text was from Gunnar. Was something wrong with Fluffy or Shadow? Had someone died? Had the beast beyond the barrier gotten through? If it were the latter, Gunnar would have had his hands too full to send me messages so I calmed my overactive imagination. I smiled as I opened it and saw pictures of a happy Fluffy, tail high in the air, and Shadow rolling around together.

I drank in the sight of them; I missed them so much. Another wave of homesickness hit me, something I'd never really battled with before. My home hadn't been all that good but now I had a home to miss, friends, too, and a boyfriend only a fool would kick out of bed. Why on earth was I stuck in stupid Sitka when all I wanted was Portlock?

Before I could second guess myself, I hit dial and rang Gunnar. 'What's up doc?' he answered and his jocular warmth flooded me.

'Hey,' I said as something in me settled. 'How are you? How's Sig?'

'We're both fine, Bunny, though we're missing our girls.'

Our girls. I grinned.

'How are you doing?' Gunnar probed.

'I'm okay. Thorsen is wearing me down.'

He grunted. 'I did some digging after you complained about him last time. For some reason I can't get his active file, but I can tell you why he has a chip on his shoulder. His dearest daddy is a senator so Thorsen has got delusions that he's somebody. That's probably why he didn't get bounced for hitting on Margilene.'

I sighed. 'It's not *what* you know, it's *who* you know.'

'You're wrong, Bunny. And you're gonna walk out of there with so much knowledge that you'll prove that to him. Chin up. You've got this.'

I swallowed past the sudden rock in my throat.

'Tell Bunny I send love!' Sigrid hollered in the background. 'And tell her we're taking great care of Fluffy and Shadow!'

'Did you hear that?' Gunnar asked.

'Hard not to.' I smiled wryly. 'She sure has a holler on her.'

'Don't I know it,' he grumbled, but the affection in his voice was clear.

'I've got to go. I just wanted to check in.'

'Sure thing.'

'Send our love to Sidnee too!' Sigrid called.

'I will. Speak soon, boss.' I rang off. *Home*: it wasn't even a place. I rolled my shoulders a few times then tackled the next message.

I grimaced: it was from my mum. I hesitated, as I had with the other thirty-plus messages she'd sent me. and in the end decided against opening it like the others. As far as I knew Mum had kept my secrets from Dad, but there was so much in my headspace right now that I didn't have room for her.

I was still processing all the hard truths about my life and the lies they'd told me, and I was still unsure about the amount of contact I wanted with her but right now the answer was a resounding zero. I was here at the academy to learn, to gain the skills for the life that I wanted, and Mum had no place here. Maybe I'd open some of her messages when I was home.

Home: there was that damned word again.

I pulled up the last message before I got too emotional. Thank all that was holy that it was from Connor; it was like he knew I needed him even when we were miles apart. I smiled and opened it.

'Oooh, that's a Connor message, I know that dreamy face,' Sidnee teased. I threw her a flat look and she laughed.

I read it quickly. *I miss you, Doe. Counting the moments.*

I smiled, though the smile faded when I realised I'd used most of my fifteen-minute break calling Gunnar and dithering about whether or not to read my mum's message. Disappointment gnawed me because there was no time left to call Connor. I'd probably just fall apart if I heard his voice for only a moment or two – it would be as cruel as giving a thirsty man only two drops of water.

Sighing, I typed a message. I aimed for some levity so he wouldn't know how much I was struggling without him. *I miss you so much. And baths. I really miss baths.*

I got an instant reply; he'd probably been watching his phone waiting for a response. *You can borrow mine any time. I adore it when you're wet.*

Some interesting places heated and a pillow hit me in a face. 'Absolutely no dirty talking while I'm here!' Sidnee said firmly.

I rolled my eyes. 'But you're always here,' I complained. 'Dorms are so shitty.'

'You're not wrong. Dibs on the toilet!' She shot off the bed and ran into the bathroom. I stowed my phone and chased her. Luckily Margi was elsewhere, so we actually got the privilege of both going at the same time. Score.

'Sig and Gunnar send love,' I said as we soaped our hands. Sidnee paused and I saw her eyes tear up in the mirror. 'Shit! Sorry,' I mumbled.

'It's okay.' She offered me a wobbly smile. 'I wasn't prepared for how much I'd miss them, you know?' She groaned. 'I even miss Stan and his terrible jokes.'

'And Thomas?' I teased.

She gave a happy sigh and a private smile tugged her lips. 'Yes, I absolutely miss Thomas.' Those two seemed to be moving at a painfully slow pace, but I guessed that with all Sidnee's traumas with her ex, Chris, Thomas wanted to make sure she had her head screwed on properly before they started something.

I thought his glacial pace might be a mistake. Sidnee was beautiful and she'd had no end of admiring glances from the other recruits. If he wasn't careful, someone else would take action before he did.

Chapter 3

The schedule at the academy was brutal. We started at 4.30am, which wasn't too bad for me because it was dark, but then the sun came up. When it was at its height, I had to fight vampire-induced daylight exhaustion all day long. That sucked because I finally got my mojo back when it was lights out at 10pm.

The last few weeks had been a battle with my very nature to function. It was fair to say I wasn't showing the academy my finest parts – though I doubted they'd appreciate my fine derrière anyway!

Everything would change when we had our 'graves' week', a full week of being nocturnal. It was designed to teach us low-light skills, which was pretty essential considering Alaska had a polar night that lasted more than two months in some places. I couldn't wait; when that started, I was going to kick so much arse.

Sidnee and I slipped into our seats moments before the class began and I opened my heavy law tome. I'd already read the section for today's lesson and, with my eidetic memory, I was pretty confident that I was well-prepared for whatever they threw at us.

We had one of the guest instructors today, Lieutenant Polk. He was a law professor who'd decided a career change was in order, thrown in a life of academia and become a state trooper. He was pushing fifty and had a receding hairline and paunch to go with it. To be honest, he looked like he'd be more suited to a cerebral life rather than running down criminals, but good on him for following his dreams.

Polk was visiting from Fairbanks and we'd had two classes with him already. He wasn't my favourite teacher because his voice droned and I struggled to focus, especially in the morning when the sun was really dragging at me and bed was calling to me repeatedly like the strumpet she was.

Polk started his lecture. Sidnee was already desperately taking notes. I took out my own notebook so I wouldn't stand out too much, but it was mostly full of doodles. I pretty much only took notes if something came to mind that I wanted to ask a question about or if I wanted to note a reference to a book in the library.

Theodore Thorsen looked over at my non-existent notes and sneered. I gave him a tight smile, friendly but aloof; I was trying to be the bigger person though I still couldn't make myself call him Theodore. 'Theodore' was an upper-class British man with a trust fund, a ramshackle castle and a rigidly determined path to his future. Thorsen was a total twat and I couldn't call him anything but that or by his surname. It wasn't likely we'd ever be on first-name terms.

I was sure that he and I would have it out before our time here was done. The fun thing was that he didn't know that he was going to lose because peds didn't have a chance against most supernats; whether he liked it or not, I was the alpha predator in this scenario. His ignorance was kind of fun. I wondered idly whether a lion ever felt smug before it pounced on a gazelle. Probably. I smiled at Thorsen. *Just call me Leona.*

The class roared with laughter. I had tuned out of the lecture so I turned to Sidnee, my eyebrows raised in question. 'Polk made a joke about the academy poltergeist stealing Jones's notebook,' she whispered.

I looked at Jones, who was behind me and two spaces to the right. I liked him; he was a nice guy, if on the shy side. He was in his early twenties like me, tall, lanky and utterly scatter-brained. I had no idea if the academy actually had a poltergeist but I was pretty sure Jones had mislaid his notebook. Again. 'Let's help him find it at break,' I whispered.

Sidnee smiled and gave me a discreet thumbs up.

I twisted in my seat and reached back to hand Jones my notebook. A lot of people needed to write stuff down for it to sink in; not me, of course, but then I'd never been 'most people', even before I'd been turned into a blood drinker.

He looked at me gratefully, took the notebook and mouthed, 'Thank you.' Thorsen glowered harder as if my kindness actively offended him. His parents must be so proud.

'That was very kind of you, Barrington, but you need to pass the test as well,' Lieutenant Polk remarked. His tone made it clear that although he thought it was *kind* he didn't think it was *smart*.

I nodded. 'Yes, sir.'

He stared at me a moment longer then turned back to the board. He continued droning on a few minutes before we got to the Q&A section of the lesson. 'Okay, let's recap. What is first-degree theft?' Polk asked.

As one, we studied the table tops; even though we were far beyond high school, nobody wanted to be marked out as a know-it-all swot.

Polk sighed. 'Anyone? Barrington?' He picked on me, no doubt paying me back for giving my notebook to Jones. He was generally a fair teacher but this call-out felt a little too pointed. Maybe I was being overly sensitive but it seemed like bullying lite – and I *hated* bullies.

Oh well. The heads-down thing wasn't working too well so maybe it was time I embraced my inner swot. I sat straight in my chair and held Polk's gaze as I recited, 'First-degree theft is a class-B felony. It consists of stealing goods, property or service at a value of $25,000. If convicted, an offender may face up to ten years in jail and $100,000 in fines.'

Polk's mouth tightened; that wasn't what he'd wanted from me. He'd wanted me to fail. What a charmer. His eyes narrowed. 'What if they have no prior convictions?'

All eyes flicked to me again; it was like a swotty version of a Wimbledon tennis match as their heads swivelled back and forth. The atmosphere was tense and Jones was looking at me with wide eyes. This wasn't what Polk had been lecturing about, but it had been in the reading that I'd dutifully devoured. 'The offender will probably be given one to three years in jail.'

Polk grunted affirmation and turned away. Sidnee nudged me with her elbow and whispered, 'Good job.' I gave her a quick smile.

I could feel the anger rolling off Thorsen and his cronies. His shoulders were tight and he twisted in his seat to glare openly at me. This time I didn't bother to smile or make nice. What was the point? He was determined to despise me no matter what I did, so I might as well embrace showing him up.

I was done with pandering to his delicate ego. I'd be civil because, thanks to my mum, manners were as much ingrained in me as speaking English, but I wasn't taking his crap anymore.

I was done playing nice.

Chapter 4

Class continued until our midday lunch break. Polk tried to trip me up one more time but lost interest when he realised I had the answers. Sidnee got one question, which she handled beautifully, and Thorsen got one that, annoyingly, he answered correctly. Poor Jones fumbled through his question and got it mostly right, but he earned another verbal jab from the lieutenant that made me fume.

I was grateful when it was time for lunch. Nobody needed me to be tired *and* hangry.

Sidnee and I hurried to our room to put away our books and for me to drink a hasty cup of blood. Since we were supernats, I was allowed a small refrigerator next to my bed to store blood. The truth about us was 'need to know', and most of the students and instructors were not 'need to know' personnel, so the rest of the staff had been told I had a medical issue and needed to keep my medicine cool.

The fridge had a combination lock so no one could open it and see rows of blood bags waiting for me inside.

Only the head of the academy, Lieutenant Fischer, and one of the instructors, Sergeant Marks, were in the know. Polk, Blake and Wilson knew nothing of the hidden supernat world, and Fischer had made it *very* clear to us on our first day that it must stay that way.

Sidnee, Margi, four male students and I were supernat recruits. Marks had commented that seven was an unusually high number for one intake because most academy cohorts only had three or four supernats, so I guessed the stars had aligned and tipped the scales in our favour. The current group, ped and supernat combined, had comprised forty students to start with although three of the peds had already dropped out.

I had a fridge but no microwave so I drank my blood cold. I tried not to gag on the thick, gloopy substance and did my thing by plugging my nose and downing it in one. Margi and Sidnee kept a lookout for me as I downed the coppery vintage. When I was done, I put the empty bag in a sealed bin marked for medical waste.

'Are you hunky-dory, Bunny?' Margi asked in her perpetually upbeat tone.

I gave her two thumbs up then the three of us headed down to the cafeteria. The blood boost had given me a little extra energy to fight the daylight fatigue that was pulling at me.

You'd have thought that the food would be institutional at a place like this but it was actually really good because a local restaurant had tendered for the catering and we were treated to bang-up meals every day. It was without a doubt my favourite thing about the academy: every day we had the choice of a sandwich, soup and salad for lunch. Today I left the salad well alone; we'd already done physical training, take-down training *and* had a lap around the obstacle course so we were all starving.

Our intake was split into four squads with ten members in each. At lunchtime we were supposed to sit with our squad for teambuilding or some such shit. Sidnee, Margi and my squads were all down a guy; the only full squad had some of Thorsen's henchmen in it and a couple of the male supernats. Harry was a caribou shifter and Eben was a witch, though I didn't know which type.

I grabbed a laden sandwich, some soup and a cup of water from the buffet then sat next to Danny, the other supernat in my squad. He was a raven shifter; the only other bird shifter I'd met was Edgy, but he didn't like to shift after he'd lost his arm in a horrible accident. Danny didn't have the same issue and every chance he got he fluttered around in bird form. I didn't blame him; I'd do the same if I could fly. Flying was cool.

'Hey, Danny, how are you today?' I asked before I bit into my turkey sandwich.

'I'm all right. I saw what Thorsen tried to do to Sidnee on the mats. She handled that well,' he said quietly.

'Yeah. He must have been a slippery baby.'

Danny burst out laughing. 'Remind me not to piss you off.'

'Don't piss me off,' I said absently then frowned. 'Still, it's a good thing she was paying attention because he could really have hurt her.' We supernats healed fast but that didn't mean that getting hurt was a walk in the park. For one thing, it really *hurt*.

When I'd been shot, I'd nearly died. Of course, that was back when we didn't know I was a hybrid with a heartbeat, and Connor and I still didn't know what that meant for my immortality. Living forever was the main perk of being a vampire; I'd be so pissed off if I guzzled blood and still aged and died after a normal lifespan. The thought of leaving Connor...

Danny picked up his sandwich. 'I heard we have a new TAC officer coming in tomorrow to replace Polk.' TAC stood for Training, Advising and Counselling. Polk may have been okay at the T part, but he sucked at the A and C. Hopefully the new guy would be better.

'Good,' I grunted. 'I don't like how Polk picks on Jones. It's not the first time he's done it.'

'I talked to him about it,' Danny admitted.

My eyebrows shot up. The balls on this guy! 'Really? What did he say?'

'I don't think Polk is a bad guy. He said he thinks it'll help Jones if he pushes him a little. I don't agree with his tactics but his heart's in the right place.'

I was impressed that Danny had called him out. Like me, Danny was already working in the Nomo's office in the other supernat village in Ugiuvak. That supernatural community was far smaller than Portlock, but Danny had the confidence of a man who knew his job and knew it well. His attendance at the academy was pretty much a rubber-stamping exercise; he sure as hell knew his shit already. I guessed he'd got the same vibe from me because we'd fallen into step from the beginning. I liked the taciturn man's hum of power; even Thorsen stepped carefully around him – another reason to hang out with Danny.

'Any idea what the new instructor will be teaching us?' I asked.

'I'm not sure but get this...' He looked around to make sure no one was listening. 'I heard he's ex-MIB.'

That caught my attention. The Magical Investigation Bureau was a wing of the alphabet agencies and largely made up of humans; they were the bogeymen who lived in our closets and under our beds. Supernat children were told toe the line or they'd be reported to the MIB, and if that happened the chances were you wouldn't be seen again, or so the stories went. However, Gunnar had a friend in the organisation so they couldn't *all* be bad – just most of them.

I licked my lips nervously. 'Are you sure?'

'Yeah.'

'Who told you that?'

'I overheard Lieutenant Fischer tell Sergeant Marks.'

I couldn't suppress a shudder. I was supposed to be tough and scary, but the MIB terrified me. A dark government entity with the job of 'watching' supernats, among other things, it felt creepy and stalkerish. I hoped the 'ex' part about the new instructor was accurate. Would he know what we were? Would he care?

I changed the topic, though I resolved to be on my guard. 'Sidnee and I are going to go look for Jones's missing notebook after we eat. Are you game?'

'Sure, I'll join in. I like the guy. He's scattered but he's smart, and he'll make a good trooper.' Like me, Danny didn't give a fuck that Jones was human; he was a good guy, no matter that he wasn't supernat.

'I appreciate that. Thanks, Danny.' I took another few bites of my sandwich. 'Since you're sneaking around and overhearing stuff, did you happen to hear any scuttle on what the next squad challenge will be?'

He laughed. 'I wish. Sorry, Bunny, I didn't hear anything useful.'

I finished my sandwich and started on my soup, glorying in not having to tip the spoon away and eat it daintily – in fact, I finished by slurping it directly from the bowl, much to Danny's amusement. 'Were you raised by wolves?' he asked.

I grinned. 'The opposite. My mum is the biggest control freak going.'

'Got it.' He paused. 'So slurping is a "fuck you" to your mom?' His grin widened. 'You know she can't see you, right?'

'It's the rest of us who are suffering,' one of the other squad members muttered.

I sniffed. 'It doesn't matter. *I* know.' I signalled Sidnee, Jones and Danny and the four of us set off to find the missing notebook. It was exciting to do something other than train; the repetitive nature of our activities was getting to me big time. I needed an adventure or I'd crack faster than a phoenix egg.

There was twenty minutes of lunchtime left and I intended to use it to solve the mystery of the missing journal. Okay, so maybe I was engineering a mystery because I was bored stiff but I didn't care.

I wanted to solve something – now. My mystery muscles were in dire need of a flex.

Chapter 5

We hastily searched the common areas then split up. Danny went to look in Jones's room, I took the classrooms, Sidnee took the gym and the mat room, and Jones scoured the break room. Nothing.

When we reconvened outside, Jones looked more downhearted than usual. It seemed increasingly likely that someone had deliberately taken the notebook to mess with him.

We had a few minutes left on the clock so we agreed to do a quick search outside. My money was on the obstacle course because we'd had a session out there during the morning's physical training session. Jones had sworn he'd had the notebook the previous night although he had denied taking it to the obstacle course.

'Sidnee, if you'll take my books to the next class, I'll do a quick run around the obstacle course,' I said.

'Are you sure?' She looked doubtfully at the clock. 'It'll be tight. You don't want to be late.'

'I'll be fast – vamp speed, if no one is looking.' I winked.

She took my books. 'Good luck!'

Sidnee and the guys had a quick look outside whilst I raced off. I sprinted to the back of the academy and scanned around each obstacle where the recruits had waited their turn. I was so engrossed that I wasn't paying attention to my surroundings.

Triumph filled me as I spied a blue notebook partially hidden under a bush. Yahtzee! As I leaned over to snag it, a foot hit me in the side and sent me flying to the ground.

I landed on the hard, cold earth with a groan, but adrenaline was pumping through me and my earlier blood boost was kicking in and I surged to my feet with inhuman speed. Before my attacker could get in another kick, I brought up my fists to protect my face like the academy had taught me. When Thorsen tried to kick me again, I blocked him easily.

Thorsen wasn't alone: three of his cronies spread out around me, faces twisted with similar expressions of hatred. Charming.

'Not so smug now, are you?' he sneered.

'I'm still a little smug,' I retorted.

He threw another punch and I blocked it again, using a little more of my vamp strength and speed. Thorsen flinched; my speed had made it a very non-human move and he'd picked up on it. At least on some level his lizard brain knew I was something to fear and that riled him to no end.

I sidestepped as he tried to grab the notebook out of my hand. Rather than engage, I spun around, ripped it from his grip and took off in the opposite direction. It meant I'd have to take the long way around the building to get to class, but I didn't want to deal with the bully and his minions.

His time was coming and I'd make sure it came like a freight train when I was well-supervised so I'd have zero black marks on my record. Thorsen's anger was easy to play with, and angry people made mistakes. As Blake loved to say, you gotta keep a level head; well, mine was as straight as a spirit level and Thorsen's was as empty as the bubble inside it. I knew I'd get another shot at him – and soon.

I slid into my seat a beat before the lecture started. The instructor was Sergeant Marks. He was average height, medium build and rather unremarkable to look at, with nondescript short brown hair and brown eyes. He knew what I was. He slid me a curious expression as he took in the notebook in my hand and the mud on my clothes, but he said nothing and got on with teaching us the ins and outs of mirandizing.

Happily, Thorsen and the others rushed in a full two minutes late, huffing, puffing and red faced. I didn't even try to stifle my smug smile. Assholes.

The academy didn't dole out punishments as such but you were expected to toe the line, so the men received a hard frown from the instructor and were given the first questions. Since they'd missed the beginning of class, they got two of them wrong and Thorsen threw me a hate-filled look that was getting old. He needed a hobby: he'd be a much nicer person if he took up crocheting and then he could get incandescent with rage every time someone mistook his work for knitting.

When Sergeant Marks' back was turned to write on the board, I slipped Jones his notebook. He gave me a bright smile and looked at me like I was the second coming. 'Thank you,' he mouthed and handed back my notebook. I'd have to photocopy the notes he'd made in it for him. I gave him a warm smile and a thumbs-up.

A sudden bang made me jump out of my seat. Annoyingly Thorsen witnessed my surprise and started hopping mockingly in his seat like he was a bunny rabbit.

He was such a wanker. I ignored him and looked around to see what had caused the ruckus.

The right-hand podium next to the flags had fallen over. I frowned as I scanned the corner and looked for the culprit who had pushed it over but there was nobody there.

'Sit down. It's either a small earthquake or Petty Peril the Poltergeist is acting up.' Teasing us with a wink, Sergeant Marks waggled his fingers as he spoke. He walked over, picked up the podium and righted it.

Titters broke out, but a chill ran down my spine. Nothing else had moved – not so much as a pencil had rolled off one of the tables – and my recent experience with various earthquakes on the Richter scale, or whatever it was called now, told me that this wasn't one. Had the podium been rigged to fall over? But why on earth would anyone do that? Besides, it hadn't *looked* rigged.

Marks knew about all things supernat so I could only assume that the poltergeist comment wasn't a joke. Many a true word spoken in jest, indeed. I caught Sidnee's eye; she'd obviously reached the same conclusion because she also looked grim. Maybe Jones *had* dropped his notebook when we were doing the obstacle course, although he said he hadn't. Or maybe...

An uneasy shiver ran down my spine. Maybe his notebook had been misplaced by a malevolent spirit. We'd had some experience with those at Portlock; even when they were ensnared in ancient jewels, the trapped banshee spirits had wreaked havoc. The experience was all too fresh and I shuddered at the thought of confronting more spirits. I didn't mind a foe I could face, whom I could reason with or punch in the face, but ghostly apparitions weren't really my jam.

I looked around, watching for any other weird movements, but nothing else happened and slowly my focus shifted back to the lesson. We practised mirandizing and moved on to the next topic but I couldn't stay focused; I kept wondering about that damned poltergeist. It seemed like I had another mystery after all.

Annoyingly, the day was packed and I didn't get the chance to pick any of the other supernats' brains. We were busy until supper; after that, when everyone else had a study period, we had our secret supernat class. It was my favourite session of the day.

Sidnee and I arrived three minutes early. Luckily the sergeant was already in the classroom so we rushed in to ask some questions. 'Sergeant, is the poltergeist real?' I demanded.

'Or an ongoing joke?' Sidnee interjected, a shade desperately. She looked more than a little nervous and alarm bells started ringing as I studied her. What experience did she have with poltergeists?

Marks looked at me first. 'Poltergeists do exist, but before today I put the occasional rumours about Petty down to some good-natured teasing.'

Sidnee and I looked at each other. 'So it wasn't a prank?' I pressed. 'The podium definitely wasn't rigged?'

He frowned and shook his head. 'No, I checked it after class. There weren't any wires or anything underneath it that could have made it fall. In fact, it's very heavy and sturdy and I struggled to push it over in the same way.' Since he was a bear shifter, that was saying something.

'Have you heard of any other strange incidents lately?' I asked.

The sergeant looked at me, amused. 'Are you missing having cases to solve?' he teased. He pressed on without waiting for a response. 'Don't worry about it, ladies. From the stories I've heard, the poltergeist is playful but not dangerous. He's nothing to worry about. Go on now, sit down. The others will be here in a moment.'

We sat down reluctantly. Clearly Marks considered the matter closed.

I slid Sidnee a look and her eyes said the same as mine: *he* might consider it closed but *we* both knew it was still as open as a frame without a door.

Chapter 6

Our supernat classmates filed in. Danny sat to my right, Sidnee to my left with Margi next to her, and Harry, Eben and George behind us in the back row.

Eben always sat at the back, and his posture and expression suggested he'd rather poke out his eyes with needles than waste his time in Marks' lessons. I guessed you'd find the lessons dull if you were raised supernatural, but for me they were fascinating and the highlight of the course. I loved learning more about magic and the community I'd found myself in.

We'd been learning about the various supernats in the 'known' population. Marks had admitted in our first lecture that a lot of the information he had was educated guesswork because each group was so secretive. He told us to take nothing as gospel, not even what he taught us. He said that our most important weapon was our gut instinct and I believed him; my gut certainly spoke to me – and some of the time it said stuff other than 'feed me'.

In the past nine weeks I'd learned about vampires, magic users and shifters, but I was still amazed by the many different supernats in the world. Today we were examining witches; they got a good amount of billing time because there were so many different types of them. I already knew about elemental and hearth witches from my short time in the Nomo's office, but they were just the tip of the iceberg. I could undoubtedly learn more if I spoke to my mother, but hey: there's a reason they say that ignorance is bliss.

What I'd learnt so far was that there was a witch for *everything*. Weather? Sure. Plants? Yep. Moon? Absolutely. Then there were forest witches and witches who had an affinity for oils and other minerals – the list went on and on. No wonder Liv strutted around Portlock like Billy Big Balls; a lot more people answered to her than I'd realised.

As the sergeant finished writing on the board, I turned to my fellow students. 'A word to the wise. Make sure you don't go anywhere alone. Thorsen found me outside and tried to beat me up. He got in a good kick before I saw him.' Marks paused for a moment before continuing to write.

Danny looked ready to spit nails so I cut him off before he could start. 'Don't worry about it. I'm already healed and I'm on the alert. There's no way he can catch me if I have room to run.'

'You need to tell Fischer. Thorsen shouldn't be able to pick on female students,' Danny growled. For a raven shifter, he sure had predator vibes.

'*Any* student,' I corrected. 'Not just female ones.' I smiled to take away any sting he might have felt from my correction.

Danny blinked. 'You're right, of course. He shouldn't be able to pick on anyone.'

'I agree. But I also need to complete this course and I don't want to get into trouble for something that no other witness can corroborate. Thorsen's goons aren't going to say anything. They didn't dirty their hands by touching me, but they stood by and did absolutely nothing.'

I frowned. 'To be honest all four of them seem to have had issues with me since Day One. I swear I haven't done anything wrong, but for whatever reason they've all been against me. Thorsen is the most vocal of the bunch and the others seem to defer to him. Anyway, don't worry. The second we have an audience I'll make sure he is seen putting the boot in.'

Danny nodded reluctantly but the other students looked sombre.

Sergeant Marks turned around and asked pointedly, 'Any questions about yesterday's lesson before we start?'

To my surprise, Eben raised his hand. 'What's the difference between an elemental witch and an elemental?'

I perked up. I'd never heard of elementals and neither had any of the others by the look of them. I had the ability to call fire, so could I be an *elemental* rather than an elemental witch? It seemed unlikely but I was happy to grasp at straws if they'd push me further from my mother's clutches. Besides, my secret hybrid status threw everything into question.

Marks perched on one of the desks and smiled. 'That's a very good question, Eben.' He clearly wanted him to engage more in the class. 'Elementals, as opposed to elemental witches, have a different source of power. Elementals draw on the actual power from the earth – water, air, fire, and earth – whereas a witch's power is innate and is drawn from their own essence.

'Some elemental witches can link to the power of the earth through charms and spells, but it's difficult except for the very strongest of them. Elementals are more powerful than elemental witches but they were nearly wiped from existence during the Dark Ages, together with other supernats. Although they're almost immortal, they don't reproduce quickly. Consequently, they keep to themselves and rarely mix with peds or others from the supernat society.'

I raised my hand and waited until Marks gave me a nod. 'Sarge, where would you find an elemental? I'd never even heard of them.'

'Why would you have, Barrington? Your records show you haven't been a supernat for very long and elementals aren't well known, even amongst supernats. They prefer a hidden existence. But have you heard of a hag or a nymph? Those are the elementals most supernats have heard about.'

I hadn't heard of hags in a supernat sense, though I'd heard old women called hags as an insult. My classmates were giving knowing nods, however.

'Hags generally live underground and are an earth-based elemental,' Marks continued. 'They have a largely humanoid appearance with the exception of their metal teeth and nails. Some have twig-like hair – but not all of them.'

I shivered: metal teeth and nails sounded threatening. I wouldn't want to bump into a hag on a dark night. Or any night, for that matter.

'Nymph is a general term for water elementals – quite a lot of lore has sprung up around them. If you know any Greek myths, you'll have heard of various nymphs. Some were even considered gods or god-like. They aren't quite as humanoid in appearance and most can't leave water, so they don't interact as often with humans as hags have in the past.'

I had heard of nymphs, nereids and naiads, so I guessed they'd had better a press than other elementals.

'Any other questions?' Marks asked.

I had thousands but I'd asked so many in each class that I let them slide for now. I didn't want my classmates to get annoyed; no one liked *that* person.

As Marks was about to continue with our lesson, Lieutenant Fischer burst in. 'Follow me!' he said urgently. 'We have a problem.'

Chapter 7

Lieutenant Fischer was a tall, striking man with a tight military haircut brushed through with silver. He was probably in his late fifties but he was still very fit. It was unnerving to see him so rattled.

The eight of us followed him into the section of the building where there were the administrative offices – and gaped at the sight that greeted us. The glass-fronted office for visiting TAC officers was in total chaos. To all intents and purposes it looked like it was in the middle of a hurricane – but one that was taking place *inside*.

'Any idea how to stop it?' Fischer asked Marks desperately.

Eyes wide, Marks shook his head. 'I'm sorry, sir. I've never seen anything like this before.'

Fischer frowned angrily. 'There's important documentation in there! He could destroy it! Help me get the door open!' He pulled down on the door handle with all of his might but he couldn't open it even an inch. Marks, Danny and George went to help but the door didn't budge even with their combined might.

'Petty Peril!' Fischer shouted, pounding on the door with his fist. 'That is *enough*!'

Everything inside the office was swirling in a violent, devastating cyclone. The desk had been knocked over, filing cabinets sent flying and huge flurries of papers were twirling around in an aerial vortex.

Fischer turned to us. 'I don't know what's gotten into him. Spread out, make sure no one human comes this way! We can't have them seeing this shitshow!'

We fanned out to check for interlopers. The other recruits were on study period and shouldn't have been out and about, so although the risk was there it was low. As far as they were aware, we were having 'remedial' lessons to bring us up to standard. It sucked that everyone thought we were failing, but we'd needed a smokescreen to hide what we were and what we were really doing in those 'extra' classes.

One of the metal filing cabinets rose up and thudded against the window, making us all duck. Luckily the glass didn't shatter, but I figured it was a close-run thing. The cabinet hit the ground with a whump and I guessed that answered the question whether the poltergeist was a threat. If anyone had been inside the office they would have been impaled by pencils and pens or battered by a freaking filing cabinet. They might have even suffered a papercut or two, and those hurt like a bitch.

I studied the angry swirl. How did you stop something invisible? I couldn't very well roll this 'Petty' onto his stomach and cuff his hands behind him.

We watched for another minute or two until suddenly everything stopped. Papers fluttered to the ground and nothing else moved. 'It's burned itself out.' Sidnee sounded grim.

I gave her a sharp look and made a mental note to question her later about her experience with poltergeists. I was sure she'd had some because her tone was so knowing.

The lieutenant went to open the door and this time it swung open. He paused cautiously, waited, and when nothing moved went inside. 'We're lucky Captain Engell wasn't in here,' he remarked. Captain Engell: that must be the name of the new TAC officer, the one Danny had said was former MIB, who was replacing Lieutenant Polk.

We filtered into the room. 'We'll have to blame vandals,' Fischer muttered, raking a hand through his shorn hair.

'We can clean it up, sir,' George volunteered. The wolverine shifter was always eager to please the officers and I wondered if it was an alpha/beta thing or a personality trait.

I helped Marks put the desk upright then we started moving filing cabinets, picking up papers and stacking them on the desk. There were tonnes of pages with random numbers on them. I was willing to bet they were the Academy's financial records and none of them would make sense when they were out of order like this, so we stacked them randomly. The filing cabinet had stayed locked, much to Fischer's visible relief, so everything was neat and tidy in short order. Someone who understood the documents would have to refile them, poor bastard.

Whilst we cleaned up, the sergeant and the lieutenant spoke in hushed murmurs in the hall. It was unnerving to see two such competent men spooked; their body language was screaming out their concern. I guessed they'd realised they were dealing with an angry poltergeist, and by their clenched jaws they didn't appear to have a clue how to do it. All aboard the novice train, it was going to be a wild ride. I should know; I'd been tooting that horn since I rolled into Portlock.

I looked at Sidnee and tilted my head towards the two whispering men. She glanced at them then looked back at me; looking grim, she nodded her assent. We had to help them get to the bottom of the ghost situation. It was time for the poltergeist to go. So far no one had been hurt but it was only a matter of time if it was ramping things up.

By the time we'd finished tidying up, our supernat class was over. I tried to hide my disappointment when the sergeant dismissed us instead of taking us back to the classroom, but at least we still had an hour left to study before lights out. We all hurried back to our rooms.

The academy's library was small but I'd have to scour it tomorrow for books on ghosts and poltergeists. In the meantime, I had a couple of other resources to tap into. I got out my phone and called Connor. 'Hey, Bunny,' he answered warmly. 'How are you?'

I sighed. 'I've been better. There's been a couple of incidents, supposedly with a poltergeist.'

'A poltergeist?' Alarm coloured his tone. 'What's happened?'

'Honestly? Nothing much so far – a missing notebook, a lectern being shoved over, that sort of thing. But the thing's just gone absolutely nuts in the TAC office. We were lucky no one was in there because they'd have been hurt – or worse.' I paused and shook my head. 'Do you know anything about poltergeists? Like how to get rid of them?' I asked hopefully. Connor had lived a longer than average life so maybe he had some insights to offer.

'I know they're not good news, but not much more than that,' he admitted. 'I've never experienced one myself. Things are quiet here at the moment so I can dig into them for you. I have some books I can look at, and I can ask Liv what she knows.'

I winced; the necromancer didn't have a whole lot of love for me since I'd arrested her ass. 'How is she doing?' I asked.

'Still keeping her head down.'

Liv had been possessed by some gemstones and under their influence she'd done some pretty damnable stuff, like seriously hurting Sigrid and Stan. She hadn't been in control of her actions, though, so she was still free to go about her business. Thinking of her gave me an idea: I'd call Father Brennan! Surely the priest could help since spirits were in *his* wheelhouse.

'Understandable. And how are you, Connor? Is everything okay?'

He laughed a little. 'Situation normal—'

'—all fucked up?' I finished with a grin. Portlock was never dull.

'You got it. It's fine, nothing to worry about. As I said, relatively quiet. I'm looking forward to seeing you.'

'Me too,' I said wistfully. 'But I'd better go. I don't have much time until lights out.'

'No problem.' He paused. 'Bunny?'

'Yeah?'

'I'll be thinking of you at lights out.' His voice was low and husky. And then he hung up.

Oh boy! I took a cold sip of water to ease my suddenly parched throat and struggled to get my head back in the game for my next two calls.

Unfortunately, Father Brennan's Irish lilt filled my ear as his voicemail told me to 'leave a message'. I did so but kept it vague. Finally I called Gunnar and was surprised – and alarmed – when Sig answered his phone. 'Hi, Bunny,' she answered with her usual maternal warmth.

I gripped the phone tighter. 'Is Gunnar okay?'

She sighed. 'He's fine but tired. With you and Sidnee both gone, he's run ragged.' I felt a surge of guilt. 'I finally persuaded the stubborn man to get some sleep and I snuck his phone away from his bedside when he was snoring. I didn't want him to be disturbed. I'm watching the office on CCTV for him tonight so April can get some downtime, too.' April Actos had been a brilliant addition to the Nomo's office; that woman was fierce.

'I'm sorry.' My voice was small.

'Now don't you go feeling guilty, Bunny! This course is necessary for your advancement. You're going to come back swinging, and Gunnar needs that from you. This is a short-term hassle for a long-term gain – it's worth it and *you* are worth it. And Sidnee is, too. I'm so proud of you both.'

The rising guilt settled. 'Thanks, Sigrid.'

'Now, what are you calling for?'

'To chat,' I lied hastily. Now that I knew Gunnar was flat out, I didn't need to add poltergeist research to his plate. Connor would come through, or maybe even the library here, and I still had Father Brennan. I had plenty of lines to tug so I could call Gunnar another time if I got desperate. 'I won't call again,' I promised Sig.

'Don't you dare stop calling!' she scolded. 'That man loves you with all of his big heart and he'd be crushed if you stopped checking in! You hear me?' Sig was a hearth witch and she was often all cuddles and gentle curves, but today her tone brooked no argument. All her softness had been stripped away to show her iron core now that she was in full protective mode. I would rather have removed my charmed necklace and stepped into sunlight than mess with her.

'Yes ma'am,' I said hastily.

'Good.' She paused. 'How's my Sidnee doing?'

I looked at my friend. Her books were spread out on her bed and she was frowning as she made notes. She was working hard and I felt another twinge of guilt: it was so much easier for me because of my ridiculous memory. 'She's doing great. Working hard, kicking butt and taking names.'

'That's my girl,' Sigrid said proudly. 'You keep an eye on each other.'

'We will,' I promised. 'Good night Sig.'

'Goodnight, Bunny. Sweet dreams.'

I slid my phone into my footlocker. 'Hey, Sidnee,' I called. 'Sigrid sends love.' I hesitated but in the end, I went for it. 'Can we talk about your experience with poltergeists?'

She froze, then buried her head in her books again. 'Not now.' Her voice was sharp. 'I'm studying. Not all of us are lucky enough to have your memory.'

Ouch. She was stressing out, so I let her snarl slide and checked the time. I had maybe half an hour left for tomorrow's reading. I pulled out the text and started to scan-read the next chapter. Who knew what sort of instructor Engell would be? If he *was* ex-MIB, I was guessing he'd be tough.

I settled into my books; I was *not* going to be found wanting.

Chapter 8

The next day started much as every day did. The monotony of the academy was one of the things that I struggled with; my Portlock life was wild and varied and no two days were the same. Being away had made me realise how much I relished the chaos.

Physical training that morning was particularly tough and I had to work at keeping my fitness within the realms of a normal human. I was dying to outperform Thorsen but I held myself back.

After a sweaty session with grumpy Sergeant Wilson, we practised takedowns. We were being tested on them soon, and I wanted to be perfect without relying on my supernatural strength and speed. Sidnee and I worked with each other for a while, then the supernat recruits and I practised together. It was so much easier to keep an extra jolt of power hidden among ourselves, plus it actually levelled the playing field since we *all* had supernatural strength and speed on our side.

Sidnee paired off with Margi whilst I went toe-to-toe with Danny. The raven shifter had a solid mass that was perfect to use against him, but sometimes when he planted his feet it was like trying to move a rock. We were both grinning as I tried – and often succeeded – to get him down.

I offered him a hand after my latest throw down. He took it and I hauled him up to standing. 'Great work,' he said, clapping me on the shoulder.

I flashed him a grin. 'Thanks!'

Danny blinked. 'Fangs!' he murmured urgently.

I hastily closed my lips over my teeth. The fuckers hadn't gotten the memo that we were messing around and must have slipped down whilst I was wrestling with Danny! I focused on calming down and pushed the excitement I'd been feeling down to a low simmer. My teeth snicked away just as Marks called together to pair us up. I got Thorsen. Yay.

'This is a test,' Marks murmured for my ears alone. 'Can you keep your cool?'

I nodded firmly and faced Thorsen. You bet your ass I could keep cool; I was going to beat Thorsen fairly and in front of lots of witnesses. I wanted to grin, but I kept it locked down in case my fangs screwed up again.

Predictably Thorsen was smirking malevolently at me. 'You're going down, little rabbit. I'll have you cuffed in ten seconds flat,' he boasted. He wasn't quiet with his smack talk and several of the other ped recruits heard him.

I rolled my eyes. 'My girl Sidnee had you on the mat in five,' I taunted. 'I think I'll be okay.' I sent him a wink designed to rile him.

That made the muscles in his jaw flex and his eyes narrow. His history suggested that he made mistakes when he got angry. He was tall, muscular and outweighed me by thirty kilos, but if the academy had taught me anything it was that winning wasn't about strength and size; it was about technique, keeping a level head and thinking on your feet.

If I could be cold and calculating under pressure, I'd stand a much better chance of not making a rookie error that would have me sailing onto the mat. Thorsen hadn't learned that yet so I had the advantage – particularly if I could get him raging. It wouldn't even be a challenge because the man was as tumultuous as a volcano when it came to me.

When we were told to start, Thorsen lunged at me with a speed I hadn't anticipated. I barely stepped out of his way in time or he would have taken me down. I berated myself, checked my ego and focused.

This time *I* approached *him* at normal human speed and he sidestepped. We circled each other. Thorsen's face was growing redder; by not being on the mat in 'ten seconds', I was humiliating him. He would lose his temper again soon and then I could totally prod him. This could be my chance for the instructors to see him deliberately hurt another recruit, but I'd have to let him follow through and actually hit me. That sucked, but I'd be fine.

First, I had to push him over the edge. 'Ten seconds?' I taunted softly, my lips barely moving.

The next time he charged me, I stepped aside but planted a hand on his back and used his momentum and a well-timed leg sweep to shove him to the ground. He went down hard with a loud oof. I deliberately didn't follow through with the cuffs but pretended to fumble them, then listened attentively to the instructor's patient explanation of what I'd done wrong. Meanwhile, Thorsen had climbed to his feet, his face purple and vibrating with rage. Perfect.

Marks had us go again and I noted Thorsen's tightly closed fists: this was the time. Ugh, it was going to hurt. When he lunged at me, I faked a stumble that put me in the path of his fist and it connected hard with my nose.

The pain exploded, as did a torrent of blood. Not even slightly faking, I cried out – it hurt like a motherfucker. But Marks had seen it and he was *furious*.

Danny pulled out an honest-to-goodness cotton handkerchief and held it to my nose. 'Thanks,' I muttered, my voice muffled.

'I promise it's clean,' he said, trying to inject some humour into the moment.

'Thank goodness for that.' I also tried for levity. 'But honestly, how old are you? Eighty? Who uses handkerchiefs in this day and age?'

He looked amused. 'People concerned with the environment.' *Touché*.

'Take her to the bathroom,' Marks instructed Margi. 'Get her cleaned up. Come back if she needs first aid.'

'Sho-nuff, sir. You can count on me, sir!' Margi said brightly.

'You!' he roared at Thorsen. 'With me!'

Margi and I trotted off. I kept the handkerchief to my face the whole time, mostly to hide the fact that I'd already stopped bleeding. We went into the nearest bathroom and I lowered Danny's snot rag. Margi winced. 'Good gravy, that must have hurt.' She blew out a breath. 'He broke your nose.'

'He *what*? That fucker!'

She studied me. 'You'll have to straighten it – and quickly – or it'll heal wonky.'

'Motherfucker.' I looked in the mirror and saw that she was right: my Greek nose was looking distinctly aquiline. I didn't really know what I was doing, but I grabbed the part that was hooked and pulled it straight. Pain exploded again and more blood spurted out. 'Ow!' I complained.

'Lordy,' Margi breathed. 'That looked painful.'

'Like you wouldn't believe,' I bitched.

Margi turned on the tap and I blinked when a stream of water flowed not straight down into the sink like gravity would dictate, but directly to me instead. I stood still as she carefully cleaned me up then turned off the tap and sent the water back to the sink. The now-bloody water drained away.

She turned to me and frowned. As a result of her ministrations, my face was cleaner but my clothes were utterly soaked. She hummed a little and the water droplets were pulled directly from my clothes and danced down the sink. Nice.

I looked at myself in the mirror. My nose was healed, the blood was gone and I didn't even have any bruising. Sometimes being a vamp was a pain – I *wanted* to look brutalised, at least for a day or two, otherwise it looked like Thorsen had only given me a damned nosebleed.

When we returned to the mat room, Thorsen and Marks were still absent. Sergeant Wilson had hastily been tagged to fill in and the dour-faced man had everyone doing drills.

Annoyingly, soon after I returned so did Thorsen and Marks. Thorsen's body language appeared contrite but his eyes were still on fire when he glanced at me. He'd had his wrist slapped and it'd had precisely no effect on him whatsoever. Marvellous.

Marks checked me over and looked relieved. I showed no signs of the blow other than the remaining blood on my gym clothes. He called us over and gave a crisp lecture about maintaining our professionalism and not allowing perps or our fellow recruits to push our buttons.

I couldn't believe it! It looked like that bastard Thorsen was going to continue his classes with no more than a telling-off, like he was a toddler that couldn't control a tantrum. Ugh. I'd have to devise a better plan, one that showed him going out of his way to hurt someone – preferably one of the supernats, since we could take it.

'You okay, Bunny?' Jones asked quietly. 'That looked like a real hefty punch.'

'He didn't pull it, that's for sure,' I agreed darkly. 'But I'm okay.'

'You're a tough cookie.' His gaze was admiring, maybe a little adoring, and he was looking at me like I'd look at a puppy. I gave him an awkward pat on the back. Whoops. It looked like my kindness to Jones had landed me with a bit of an infatuation. I'd have to make sure to let him down gently because I was all fixed for a boyfriend.

Thinking of Connor made my heart twinge. God, I missed him more than scones and jam. I couldn't finish the course quickly enough.

Chapter 9

Captain Engell dealt with the financials for the school and taught a few classes when he wasn't in Anchorage doing his regular trooper job; lucky him, he was our instructor for the morning session.

The atmosphere was tense; we were obviously divided between those who thought Thorsen was a hero and those who thought he was a pillock. I was pleasantly surprised to find myself surrounded with plenty of people – peds *and* supernats – who were willing to offer me their support and send a clear message to Thorsen that his behaviour would *not* be accepted.

I watched Engell as attentively as I could, given the depth of boredom his material inspired in me. He was probably in his early forties, dark-haired and muscular; if he'd retired from the MIB, he didn't look like any retiree I'd ever seen before. His eyes were dark and brooding and, despite the unholy level of tedium in his class, there was something that felt inherently dangerous about him. As he stalked around the classroom, it felt like being in the zoo next to a tiger which, frankly, felt like a bad idea.

Engell was teaching us a mini-clinic on forensic accounting. If he was, or had been, MIB, he was surely the most boring of the lot of them. My eyes nearly rolled up in my head as he spoke and I struggled to keep them open. His teaching style left much to be desired – he even made Polk seem animated – but he seemed knowledgeable. Most importantly, he didn't bully Jones.

An hour into class, when most of us were struggling to stay awake, the same podium fell over again with a bang and jolted us all awake. The poltergeist didn't stop with that, however; all our papers, pens and pencils were sent flying directly at the hapless instructor. Engell ducked behind his podium; the clatter of instruments striking it and the board behind him was like the noise of a hailstorm.

'Someone shut the damned window!' he shouted. Danny hastily stood, but he waited until the poltergeist had dissipated before sliding closed the fractionally open window.

Engell stood up. If he knew about the paranormal world, his slightly stupefied expression didn't convey it. Either that or he was a pretty good actor.

'Are you okay, sir?' Thorsen asked with surprising concern. Maybe even he could show some empathy now and again, though the cynical part of me suspected he was brown-nosing.

'You wouldn't think the wind could come through with such force,' Engell muttered. 'I only opened it a little for some fresh air.' Nobody pointed out that the trees outside were wholly still. He was bleeding from various superficial cuts so we took a quick break whilst he cleaned himself up, then he continued his lousy lecture like nothing had even happened.

When the lecture finished, we were divided up and taken to either the gun range or the obstacle course. My squad and Sidnee's were at the range.

Unlike the revolver that Gunnar had started me with, the academy used Glock 17s. It was a commonly used police gun, though I hadn't shot one before. It was a different experience because the safety mechanism was built into the trigger. The advantage was that it was far faster in an emergency since all you had to do was point and depress the trigger fully to get it to work.

Since I'd been practising regularly with Gunnar, I was a decent shot and sailed through my turn. I had started to really enjoy shooting because it was the one exercise where your skill wasn't dependent on your physical strength; with a gun in my hand, I didn't have to hide anything.

Sidnee wasn't keen on shooting but she'd been around Gunnar since she was seventeen so she knew how to do it. She aced her turn, too.

We rotated through our shotgun and rifle time. The academy used Remington 870s and Colt AR 15s, which were fun to shoot. We had the same models back at the Nomo's office though I'd yet to see them out of the gun safe since the werewolf incident.

It was bizarre to think how far I'd come from being a Brit who'd never held a gun to being comfortable firing a variety of weapons. I was proud of me, even if my parents wouldn't ever be. I squelched the thought: there was no time for self-pity.

Just before lunch we were told about our second squad challenge. Squad challenges were designed to be fun, team-building exercises that earned us minor rewards. They also allowed those of us who were a smidge competitive to let off steam and had the extra benefit of earning us some cohort kudos, as well as some time off campus.

The challenge was scheduled for after lunch. We had to go into Sitka, locate five different totem poles, have a squad photo taken with each of them, then return to the academy. Whoever returned first with the photos won an extra hour's sleep in the morning and could skip physical training. An hour extra in bed was a small thing to look forward to – but I mostly wanted to make sure Thorsen didn't win it. Yes, I was *that* petty.

If the supernats had made up a squad we'd have won easily, but we were split amongst the four squads so it was equal footing. The squads were divided as much as possible between men and women. My squad put together a plan during lunch; it looked like today I was having grilled-chicken pasta salad with a side of sneaky strategy.

As we finished eating, we agreed to go and get our phones. I ran up to my room, flung myself on the bed and reached for my phone in my footlocker. As my fingers closed around the device, the hair on the back of my neck stood on end and anxiety curled in my gut – together with the certainty that I wasn't alone. *Trust your gut.*

There was a shadowy figure in the corner of the dorm. It was roughly human shaped, although its features were somehow obscured. My brain tried to fill in the features but failed, and a shiver of fear ran down my spine.

I pushed myself up to a sitting position, feet on the floor, ready to fight – or to run.

As my nerves stretched taut, a series of low moans came from the apparition. My sharp hearing could almost pick up words but I couldn't quite make them out; it was like there was some weird disconnect between my ears and my brain.

As I continued to sit there, staring stupidly and not responding, the spirit grew agitated. It spoke again more forcefully but I still couldn't understand it. All traces of fear left my body as I concentrated on its desperate attempt to communicate. Regretfully I shook my head. 'I'm sorry. I can't hear you.'

Frustrated, it swirled around the room and under a bed at the far end. The bed lifted three feet off the ground and slammed back down, and a foul scent like rotting eggs and meat filled the air. The ghost rushed towards me and then vanished.

My lethargic heart gave a solid thump as I tried to analyse what had just happened. For some reason my lizard brain hadn't been afraid. *Trust your gut.*

Right. Well, the weird thing was that my gut was saying that maybe the poltergeist wasn't as malevolent as we'd thought…

Chapter 10

I wiped my hands down my uniform pants and hurriedly grabbed my phone, shifting my eyes around the room in case the poltergeist came back. I wished I had time to talk with Sidnee but she was meeting with her team.

I pulled myself together, hurried down to join my squad and together we hit the ground running. We were now equipped with Satnav, should we need it; there were no express rules against it, so at least we'd know where we were going if we were somehow separated.

Jones, who was in our squad, was local and he knew where to find five of the closest totem poles. Over lunch he'd sketched out a route for us to take. Another of Blake's golden nuggets was that having a local was a real advantage; one of our earliest lessons was about using local intel. There was a reason law enforcement often used confidential informants.

We set off under Jones' direction. It was over a mile jog but we were relatively fresh; even so, I constantly had to remind myself to stay in the middle of the pack to avoid suspicion. My ego wouldn't let me run at the back, but I happily kept pace with Danny. Jones, whose lanky build hid a competitive long-distance runner, took the lead easily. He was almost visibly increasing in confidence as we moved.

We had one of Thorsen's besties in our squad, Frederick Miller, and I watched him doing his level best to keep up with Jones. Presumably he'd intended to be the front runner but Jones' long strides stopped him. I kept a cynical eye on Miller; I wouldn't have been at all surprised if Thorsen hadn't given him instructions to sabotage our group. Hopefully Miller's self-interest would win out, though I wouldn't have bet on it.

As we trotted to our first totem pole, my phone vibrated with a text from Connor. I suppressed a girlish squeal of delight and checked it.

I emailed you what I could find about poltergeists. Most of the lore is vague, so not a lot of good info. I'm still digging into it. Love you.

Love you, I tapped back, keeping my response short since texting while jogging was surprisingly hard. I was salivating to check my emails and dive into the information, but this was one of the times where I needed to live in the moment. I was in the middle of a competition and pride wouldn't allow me to give it less than a hundred percent.

I slipped my phone back into my pocket and pushed a little harder to catch up with Danny. He gave me an inquisitive look. 'Boyfriend,' I said.

'Ah.' Danny was a chatty soul.

It started to rain. It could rain here even in late autumn but that was better than ice or snow. I should have been better prepared: oh well, I wouldn't melt.

We ran faster and soon saw the first totem pole. Jones arranged us and I asked a tourist to take our squad photo with my phone, then we were off to totem number two. Jones had taken us into the Sitka National Historic Park where there were a lot of totem poles, so luckily, it was close by.

We rushed through the park, successfully hitting pole after pole. With all five photos secured, we started back towards the academy at top speed – top *human* speed. As we were leaving the park we passed another squad that had evidently had the same idea, but the other two teams were nowhere to be seen. Fingers crossed they hadn't got back before us; I could really use that extra hour to investigate what the fuck was going on with that damned poltergeist.

Happily, we beat Thorsen's squad to win the contest by three whole minutes. I couldn't restrain my victory dance; I was more than willing to shove our success in his face, one wild hip gyration at a time. Yes, I was provoking him but he did stupid things when provoked and getting him kicked out of the academy was almost as much a target of mine as finding out about poltergeists and successfully completing the programme.

We had won the extra hour in the morning and I intended to make the most of it in the academy library. My squad's spirits were high and almost all the other recruits congratulated us on our victory when we ate together. I felt warm and fuzzy when people took the time and effort to speak to Jones personally and praise him for his leadership. Clearly I wasn't the only one who had a soft spot for the timid guy.

Dinner ran over and evening study was cancelled. I should have been cheering, but losing another supernat lesson stung. I did my best to paste on a happy face and mingle. When we were finally released back to the dorm, I pulled out my phone. I had two options: read Connor's email or speak to the man himself. A second later I was dialling his number.

The phone rang twice before he picked up. His warm voice sent all kinds of fluttering to my belly. 'Bunny!' he said, then a deeper, huskier, 'I miss you.'

'I miss you too.' And I did. There was an ache in my stomach, a yearning I couldn't shake. Our nascent bond didn't like us being apart for long. Nor did I.

'I have a surprise cooking up for you, Doe.'

My eyebrows shot up. What kind of surprise could he get to me while I was here? I considered the possibility that he might be sending me a care package since we were allowed those, but then it occurred to me that the Commander's Weekend was fast approaching – a whole three days off. We had to stay on the island but there was no PT, no classes. A buzz of excitement hit me. If I was wrong with my deduction and all Connor was sending me were some more teabags, I'd be gutted.

'Are you coming to see me?' I squealed. Oops, I took a breath and tried to chill; squealing was unbecoming in a detective.

Connor's chuckle rumbled through the tinny phone speaker and I pictured leaning against his chest as it against vibrated me. Yum. 'I can't fool a detective!' he teased. 'But there's more to it than that, and there's no way you'll deduce this one so you'll have to wait.'

Waiting was not my strong suit, though I'd got better at it during the last few weeks. 'Hurry up and wait' was not only a mantra in the British military but also in the Alaska State Troopers. Every morning after PT it felt like the next class was always deliberately held up to keep us waiting; standby to standby, indeed.

Still, if Connor wanted to surprise me I would let him. I did my best to relax and tried to ignore any changes in the timbre of his voice. 'How are Fluffy and Shadow?' I asked.

'They're fine,' he reassured me. After a pause, he addressed the question I really wanted to ask. 'Reggie is still struggling with holding his human form so he rarely shifts – he seems happier as Fluffy. Only Gunnar seems to make him comfortable enough to take on his human skin.' He sounded mildly amused and a little exasperated. 'And Shadow is Shadow. He does whatever he wants and gets mad if you don't think he's cute while he's doing it.'

I laughed. No matter what kind of supernatural being he truly was, Shadow was most definitely a cat. 'Thanks for that.' I sighed. 'I don't have much time. I'm still trying to dig into the poltergeist thing and I haven't even had a chance to read your email yet.'

'No problem, I'll give you the highlights – though I'll start with the disclaimer that there is a lot of conflicting information out there. Some sources say you can get rid of a poltergeist –or at least calm one down – by cleansing the area it haunts. They are thought to be negative spirits so negative energy feeds them. Whatever you do, keep that sunny personality beaming.'

I laughed; I was a lot of things but sunny wasn't one of them. Were the incidents somehow my fault? Was I feeding the poltergeist with my negative feelings towards Thorsen? God knows, I'd had plenty of them.

Connor continued, 'I've emailed you a list of things to do for the cleansing. I won't repeat them because there's a bunch of steps and I'd definitely screw up the order. And don't forget that I'm getting this info from dubious websites – there no guarantee any of it will work.'

My hopes diminished a little; I'd been hoping for a step-by-step, 100% effective solution that took only five minutes and totally obliterated the poltergeist. 'No Liv?' I asked softly.

He hesitated. 'She's not playing ball. I'll keep trying.'

Despite myself, my stomach lurched. A non-compliant Liv was a tricky Liv. I bit my tongue before I could warn him to be careful; he knew Liv better than I did, and he knew he had to tread carefully. 'Thanks for all of this. I know you're busy,' I said instead.

'It was a quick read of a few books and a web search, not an international spying investigation,' he teased. 'It was no bother.'

'Even so, I'm grateful.' I smiled. 'I'll show you how grateful I am at the Commander's Weekend.'

His voice was warm when he replied, 'I'm counting down the hours.'

So was I.

Chapter 11

I finally read Connor's fifteen-page email; he hadn't been kidding about conflicting information. Huffing, I stuffed my phone back in the footlocker. Sidnee was watching me, amused. 'Connor and Bunny, sitting in a tree...' she started singing.

'Yeah, yeah.' I rolled my eyes at her before sobering. 'Sidnee, hun, it's time to spill.'

She looked confused. 'What?'

'What experience do you have with poltergeists?'

She froze. 'How did you know I have any?' she prevaricated.

I gave her a flat stare. 'Well, mostly from the hints you keep dropping, stuff like "it's burned himself out." You're in the know, Sidnee, and I need to know too.'

She looked away. 'I don't like to talk about it,' she said finally. 'It was a very scary time in my life and I try very hard to pretend none of it happened. It's a dark chapter in my family's history.'

I crossed the distance between us and settled on her bed. 'Look, I'm sorry to make you talk about it but I really do need to know.' I told her what Connor had said and pulled up his email of conflicting instructions. 'All this is contradictory, and I have a source with real experience right next to me.'

'What about Father Brennan?' she tried.

'I've already called him and left a message. He hasn't picked it up yet – at least, he hasn't replied. You're all I've got, Sid.'

She sighed. 'Fine. I was twelve, in the Philippines. This was before my parents died, and my grandmother and uncle were still alive. We had to leave our house for a few weeks because we were replacing the pipes or something like that. It doesn't matter.' She waved it away. 'Anyway, we moved into my grandmother's house. It wasn't very large and my uncle was living there too, so the only place for me to sleep was in an alcove off the kitchen. They put up a little cot bed for me.'

I leaned forward, silently encouraging her to tell me more.

'Nothing happened the first night – at least, I didn't notice anything. Then there were a few weird things, but nothing you'd really consider *off*, you know?'

I didn't so I shook my head. 'No. Like what?'

She picked at her dark-blue bedspread. 'Things like you'd set something down and it would disappear, only to show up in a strange place. Or the kitchen cabinets would be open in the morning but no one remembered leaving them that way. My uncle was drinking a lot so we put it down to him. He was stuck in a vicious cycle, often drunk or hungover.'

'I'm sorry you had to see that so young,' I murmured.

'Yeah, it was an eye-opener.' She sighed. 'Then things got progressively worse. A pan would fly off the stove towards us all. Doors would slam. The atmosphere got tense and we started to think it really was a ghost. I tried to talk to it, to tell it to calm down, but that seemed to make it madder or give it power.'

She'd gone pale and her hands were shaking – I was forcing her to talk through some real shit here. I reached out to pull her into a hug and rubbed her back. I could feel the tension in her muscles. 'I'm sorry, Sidnee. This is horrible. You don't have to talk about it. I'll figure it out. I shouldn't have pressured you.'

She shook her head, pushed me away and took a deep breath. 'No, I'm being dumb. You need to know what happened – what *could* happen. My uncle and I were going down the stairs and it shoved him. He knocked into me, and I fell down the stairs and sprained my ankle quite badly. At that point we were all freaking out. We were terrified to stay in the house.'

'I'm so sorry.'

'Yeah. So my grandmother called in a priest.'

'Was she Catholic?' I asked, thinking of Father Brennan. The dominant religion in the Philippines was Roman Catholic. She nodded but, lost in her memories, she didn't speak for a moment.

I prompted, 'Did the priest get rid of it?' If so, I was going to start hounding Father Brennan.

She shrugged. 'He seemed to because all the activity stopped for a time. But then it came back even worse, like we'd made it even madder. By then we'd moved back to our own house, but my grandmother refused to be driven out of her home and she and my uncle stayed there.' She licked her lips. 'Until one day it pushed my uncle down the stairs again and this time it snapped his neck. After that, Grandma came to live with us, but I'm sure the stress and the death of one of her sons led to her early death.'

I squeezed her hand gently. 'God, that's awful. I'm so sorry, Sidnee.'

She gave a sad smile. 'It was a long time ago. After my uncle died, the police found his partial fingerprints in the system. It turned out he was a serial rapist. His death led to a lot of cold cases being solved.'

I gasped, feeling at a total loss. I wanted to say something comforting but I had absolutely nothing. That was *horrible.*

Sidnee gave a bitter smile. 'I told you it was a dark time. The police guessed that one of his attacks had gone further than usual and the poor girl had died. He'd buried her in the garden and she'd taken up residence in my grandmother's house as a poltergeist. She'd grown in power until she'd killed my uncle – and after that she left. But the truth of my uncle's darkness killed Grandma as much as his death. Poltergeists scare me, Bunny, with damned good reason.' She looked me straight in the eye. 'We have to get rid of this one. Before it kills someone.'

No shit. Her tale made my radar hum. She might not have noticed it but her story painted the poltergeist not only as the killer but also as a victim, and something about the apparition's desperation when it had appeared to me had suggested the same.

If that were true, who did it want to wreak vengeance on? Because my money was currently on Engell.

Chapter 12

Connor's email had a bunch of actionable tips, one of the most obvious of which was the practice of sageing. The problem was that I couldn't leave the building so close to lights out to find some white sage or any of the other things he'd mentioned, so that was out for now. However, Sidnee was friendly with one of the dinner ladies and said she'd try and scrounge some from the kitchen when she could.

Apart from the sage, one of the other things was the prayer to Saint Michael. I could have used my hour to sneak into every unoccupied common space and recite it, but Sidnee's story gave me pause. Her family had tried to get rid of their poltergeist, and whatever the priest had done had made it disappear temporarily, but it had returned with a vengeance. I didn't want to force our poltergeist to up the ante and become even more violent.

I wished there was a way to communicate with the ghost but I had zero experience with summoning spirits. I froze at that thought; I didn't have *zero* experience because I'd summoned Aoife on several occasions. Could she come to me this far away from Portlock? She had managed to communicate with the spirits in the gemstones – though admittedly they were banshees like her. Even so, it was definitely worth a shot. If Aoife could communicate with other spirits, maybe she could ask our poltergeist to stop!

I decided to use my free hour the following morning to try and speak with Aoife. If that didn't work, I could always go back to the original plan of going to the library. Satisfied, I rolled over to my side and drifted off to sleep.

When I awoke, I completed my morning routine and waited until Sidnee and Margi had left for PT. I didn't need witnesses if this all went pear-shaped.

Finally alone, I sat on my bed, crossed my legs, closed my eyes and looked inwards for any sort of connection that I had with Aoife. Predictably I found nothing; we didn't have a bond like me and Connor. Even so, I had to try. 'Aoife,' I said loudly, 'I need your help. Please come to me.'

I opened one eye: nothing. I sighed, closed my eyes and tried again, injecting a little more force into my voice. 'Aoife Sullivan!' I called sharply, then I entreated, 'If you can travel this far, please come, Aoife.'

The wheedling tone clearly worked because I felt a wave of freezing cold air. I opened both eyes and Aoife was standing before me, her colourless hair floating about her in an invisible wind. Like a typical teenager, she'd assumed a pouting position: arms folded across her chest, hip cocked, flat look. She didn't say anything, although I knew she could. She was a really strong banshee.

'Thanks for coming, Aoife.' I shot her a grateful smile. 'I really need your help. We have a problem here, a poltergeist that's started to become violent. I was hoping you could talk with it and see if there's a way to get it to stop.' Her stance relaxed and I wondered what she'd been expecting me to ask of her. 'Can you help?'

She shrugged and I waited. When she opened her mouth I tensed, expecting her banshee wail to unnerve me as it had so many times before. Sure enough, the cold intensified and her screeched words made me want to clamp my hands over my ears. 'I've never met a poltergeist. I cannot promise anything.'

Something about her voice pierced my very soul. 'I don't have any other options. Please can you try?' She gave an abrupt nod and disappeared. I breathed a sigh of relief. Maybe this whole situation could be resolved quickly.

I waited for a few minutes for her to return but she didn't. I didn't want to waste the rest of my precious hour so I took my laptop to the library as I'd originally planned. Rather than looking for general information on poltergeists, I decided to see if I could find out anything about this specific one, Petty Peril. I assumed that was a corruption of his true name; Peril may well be his real surname, but I was guessing that Petty was probably Peter or something similar.

I really needed to access the records of staff and past recruits because it seemed likely that someone had died at the academy. Maybe their body was buried here, like Sidnee's uncle's victim.

There was no sign of any records in the library – they were probably confidential and locked away in a database – so I sat at my computer and signed into the slow library Wi-Fi. Once I was connected, I searched for deaths that had happened in or around the academy during the last few years. Nothing.

I extended the search parameters and finally I found something from thirty years ago.

After a three-day search, a recruit, Petrovich Peril, was found. It appears he had become lost and confused while hiking in the woods and had died of exposure. Our condolences are with the family over this tragic loss. The State Trooper Academy has closed for one day to allow his friends and acquaintances to attend the funeral. The family has requested that flowers and donations are sent to...

This was it, a short, emotionless obituary in the local paper, but at least I had his true name. I'd never have guessed Petrovich, but there was a lot of Russian influence in this part of Alaska so I guessed it made sense.

I filed the information into my memory and checked my watch: my time was almost up. I hurried back to my dorm and put away my computer. As I closed my footlocker, an icy breeze washed over my skin and I looked up. Aoife was hanging in the air next to me. 'How did it go? Did you have any luck?' I asked hopefully.

I braced myself for her banshee-wail reply.

'He is angry. Someone is trying to harm the academy. He is trying to draw attention to it.'

I frowned. Harm the academy? I thought that Thorsen was at risk of harming the academy's *reputation*, but although he'd been present at a few of the episodes he hadn't been attacked – not like Engell. 'Did he say who? Or what is being done?' I pressed. Engell dealt with financials and I'd seen the pages of numbers floating around. Could he be embezzling from the academy?

Aoife shook her head. 'It's tough for us to communicate, like we are on different frequencies. What I managed to get was garbled. He isn't trying to hurt anyone. He has the academy's best interests at heart, but someone here doesn't. That was all I got. You need to find a way to communicate with him because he was reluctant to speak to me.'

'Thank you, Aoife. Your help has been invaluable.' I frowned. 'It's weird that he's trying to help when he's done a lot of damage and someone could have been hurt.'

She shrugged then faded from view. I yelled, 'Bye, Aoife!' after her, but I wasn't sure that she heard – or cared. Still, manners were important.

I thought about what I'd learned because it changed everything. If the poltergeist was trying to *help* the academy, then who was trying to bring it down? And why?

Something fishy was going on, and I was determined to get to the bottom of it.

Chapter 13

I only had fifteen minutes left of my free hour. I pelted down the stairs at full vampire speed figuring that nobody would see me dipping into my supernat powers whilst they were at PT.

Recruits weren't allowed in the administrative office but I was hoping that the staff would be busy elsewhere. I glanced in casually and grinned when I saw that the office was empty. So far, so good. I slipped through the casement of the receptionist's window and went to the TAC officer's bureau where we'd witnessed Petty's temper tantrum.

The office was immaculate. We'd helped clean it up but had left most of the organisation to our visiting TAC officer, Captain Engell, who was apparently a neat freak. Everything was precisely so, with nothing extraneous on his desk: he'd gone full minimalist. I bet he only had one book by his bedside at a time and shuddered at the thought.

I checked the time on my phone then started searching. The desk was an old, wooden kneehole design with a long narrow drawer for pens and whatnot, and three sets of drawers down each side. The bottom left and right drawers were locked but I found a likely looking key in another drawer. Bingo!

Predictably, the left-hand file drawer was full of files and they were all financial. I wasn't surprised since Captain Engell did the academy's books as well as teaching several classes. Although I wasn't sure what I was looking at, I took the time to scan-read several of the files, putting them into my memory so I could examine them properly later.

The right-hand drawer was completely empty and there was no sign of dust. That piqued my interest: where were the documents that had resided here? I closed and locked it, then turned my attention back to files in the left-hand drawer. Annoyingly I ran out of time before I ran out of files, so I hurriedly relocked the drawer and sneaked out of the office.

I made it back in time for flag formation. Afterwards I used a little more vamp speed to run upstairs to my room and slug back my blood before hurrying to the cafeteria where I was expected to be for breakfast.

Frustratingly, despite my extra-curricular activities I wasn't that much further along. I now knew that the ghost was protecting the academy – but I had no idea from what.

I joined my squad with a full breakfast plate. They all looked well rested because they'd used their extra hour to sleep in, the jammy gits. Oh well: I was always tired during the day so the extra hour probably wouldn't have helped much. I was looking forward to the week of night drills when the schedule flipped and I'd finally get decent day sleep like a good little vampire.

I looked around the room for Sidnee and she gave me a wave. I joined her for class as usual, and we settled down for an in-depth lecture on DV: domestic violence. Fischer himself was giving the class, which only served to show how important the topic was to the academy. What was surprising – though perhaps it shouldn't have been – was that DV wasn't always a man hurting a woman but also vice versa. There was also a huge psychological component to it that I hadn't really been aware of.

'From the outside it's easy to query why the victim didn't leave their abuser,' Fischer said. 'Have you heard of Stockholm syndrome?' We all nodded. 'Good. Jones, what is it?'

Jones cleared his throat and looked mildly anxious at being called on by the head of the academy. 'Stockholm syndrome is a psychological response in which a person being held captive forms a bond with their captor. This bond can lead the victim to develop loyalty or even affection for the person hurting them, sometimes to the point of refusing to cooperate with authorities against their captor. It develops as a coping mechanism because the victim's mind seeks to find some level of safety or stability in an otherwise terrifying situation.'

Looking pleased, Fischer nodded. 'You absolutely nailed that, Jones. You're right. The same thing applies to victims of domestic abuse who often want to protect their abuser, which makes arresting that abuser a heck of a lot harder. Many victims are told repeatedly that everything is their fault, that they are responsible for every hit, every punch or kick. They believe that their own behaviour *caused* the abuse and, as a result, they don't think the perpetrator is actually guilty of anything at all.

'It will take time and a whole lot of understanding to get the victim to open up, let alone press charges. You have to be patient and conduct multiple interviews before the majority of victims even start to talk about these things. During those interviews, you mustn't show your frustration or your anger at their situation. Any hint of aggression and they will close down and clam up – they'll put you in the same category as the offender. You will be deemed not trustworthy and also potentially dangerous.'

It surprised me to see Thorsen nodding seriously. His notebook was open and he was taking a lot of notes. Maybe he wasn't a *total* douche-canoe.

Fischer continued, 'If you can, it's often best to get a female officer to talk to the victim.' He held a hand up to stop the questions as hands were raised instantly. 'I'm not saying that because the victim is more likely to be female but because, whether you like it or not, women come across as being less aggressive and more empathetic. Even male victims sometimes prefer speaking to a female officer, though I have had occasions when male officers have been requested. Regardless, whoever interviews must be calm, quiet and attentive. You must *listen*. You should *never* interrupt.'

He paused. 'If you take nothing else from the course, remember this: there are occasions where you should SHUT UP and LISTEN. Am I clear on that?'

We nodded. 'What should you do?' he asked again, eyeing us all.

'Shut up and listen,' we chorused back.

'That's right.' Fischer moved on to practical issues – for example, most victims wouldn't want the interview to be recorded in case their abuser got a hold of the tape – then talked about how such cases might affect us. He flagged up the need to assess our own mental health, particularly after dealing with particularly difficult or triggering cases. Some of the case studies he ran through were enough to make me feel physically sick. The whole class had been a real eye opener.

Finally we did some role-play and it was good to see everyone taking it really seriously. By the end of the morning's session, I felt a lot more prepared to deal with DV, though I hoped I wouldn't have to because it made me think darkly of my sire, Franklin, and how different life might have been if I'd bowed to his demands and joined the conclave. Knowing about Stockholm Syndrome had me considering that episode in a new light; I doubted it would have taken me the full one hundred years to get indoctrinated into worshipping the vampire king.

I shuddered. Running away to Portlock was the best thing I'd ever done.

Chapter 14

At lunchtime the scuttle amongst us supernats was that no further poltergeist activity had been seen. Maybe speaking to Aoife had exhausted it, I thought hopefully. Maybe her words had made it rethink its actions.

Unfortunately it struck again, halfway through the DV class after lunch. This time, instead of attacking our instructor or knocking over a podium, it marched the two flags that were sitting up front around the room like little skinny soldiers then flung them on the floor.

'The windows are closed,' Jones said into the tight silence. 'It wasn't a breeze that made them do that.'

Fischer laughed and picked up the flags to put them back in their stands. 'Okay, recruits, our resident ghost Petty Peril is blowing off some steam. Nothing to worry over. Let's get back to work.'

We looked nervously at each other and started whispering. No one minded ghosts in theory, but for the humans in the room this was an unwelcome suggestion that something beyond their understanding truly did exist.

Fischer had complete control of the room; when he held up a hand we fell silent for him to continue his lecture as if nothing had happened. I tuned into his words and forced myself to think of something other than the damned poltergeist.

As the lecture ended, my attention wandered and I started thinking of other things I could do to further my investigation. I wanted to go back to the TAC officer's room and do some more sleuthing to see if I could find a file on Petrovich.

My ears pricked up when Fischer said something about Commander's Weekend, and my floppy heart fluttered a moment in my chest. Connor was coming to see me – and soon! This coming weekend! Hearing it announced made it more real and I could hardly wait.

After class, Sidnee and I walked to supper with the other supernats and I brought them up to speed about Aoife's conversation with Petty. I figured they could help look for anything that was putting the academy in danger.

'What kind of danger?' Danny asked.

'I don't know. The answers were vague – apparently poltergeists aren't that chatty. My banshee said they spoke on a different frequency so communication was a bit shambolic.'

'Did Petty say who is to blame? Who we should be watching?' Eben pried.

I sighed. 'I don't know,' I said again, 'but it makes sense that we should check out the new TAC officer, since his office was targeted and he was attacked. But I also think we should look at any shifty recruits like Thorsen. This violent behaviour is new, which suggests that whoever is causing it is a new arrival. Hey, Margi, you and Eben are witches. Do you know any way to speak to, or diminish, the poltergeist?' I wanted to give myself a face palm that I hadn't thought to ask earlier.

'No, sorry. I'm an elemental water witch,' Margi said. 'Maybe an air witch could do something, but I've never been taught anything about ghosts. All I know about them is from the movies.'

'I'm a shaman, not a witch,' Eben said sourly. 'Ghosts aren't my thing.'

'Sorry, my mistake,' I said faintly. I could have sworn that he'd introduced himself as a witch – and when I searched my memory, sure enough that was *definitely* how he'd introduced himself.

Why would he lie? A shaman was totally different to a witch. Had he felt pressured or awkward because there were no other shamans on the course? Maybe he'd blurted out 'witch' to fit in with Margi, but now felt comfortable enough to tell the truth? Either way, it was weird.

Eben was from a small village up by Nome and, like me and Sidnee, he already had a job: he was a VPSO, a Village Public Safety Officer. There were village police officers from all over Alaska here at the academy for training so they could go back home all polished and up to date.

He went on, 'We have some rituals for hauntings, but I'll have to consult with my elders at home. It might take a while to get the stuff we need, but I'll do my best.'

'Thanks!' I said brightly. 'Let us know when you get a hold of someone.'

He mumbled indistinctly. As soon as the other supernat recruits joined in and we were talking about our training experience and how hungry we were, I sidled up to Sidnee. 'Eben totally introduced himself to me as a witch,' I said in a low voice.

She looked surprised. 'Are you sure? He definitely said he was a shaman to me.'

I rolled my eyes. 'Of *course* I'm sure.'

'Oh right – freaky memory.' She frowned. 'Maybe it's because vamps and shamans don't always get on? Mers and shamans don't have any issues, so maybe that's why he told me the truth but not you?'

'Maybe,' I conceded as I checked my memory again. Sure enough, I'd introduced myself as a vampire before Eben had said anything about himself. 'Vamps don't get on with shamans?' I queried. Anissa in Portlock had never shown me anything other than kindness.

Sidnee grinned. 'It's not a specific feud or anything, and it's not as bad as werewolves and vamps! I think maybe vamps don't really like *anyone* except other vamps and it shows.'

'I like plenty of other supernats,' I protested.

She laughed. 'You're an anomaly.'

Oh yay, lucky me.

The funny thing was, she was even more right than she knew.

Chapter 15

Things were quiet leading up to Commander's Weekend; even the poltergeist and Thorsen were creepily quiet and I couldn't help but feel it was the calm before the storm. Even so, I was grateful because I *really* wanted the weekend to go off without a hitch. I would spit nails if something interfered with me seeing Connor; the need to be in his arms was almost like a physical ache.

The week seemed to drag interminably and I was also feeling rather down on myself for not having solved the mystery of whatever the fuck was going on. Luckily we'd had a strenuous set of classes to keep me busy, including taser and expandable-baton training on top of our theory lessons. What they didn't tell us beforehand was that we had to experience all the modes of control before we got to use them. Believe me, being tasered hurt like a bitch; I definitely wouldn't be doing it to anyone else willy-nilly.

By Thursday we were all bruised and tired. Blood took care of my injuries but I felt bad for my shifter and magic-user friends. The shifters rarely found the time and space to shift, except for Danny who couldn't resist flying around his dorm room at night, and the magic users couldn't find the time and ingredients to brew up a potion to fix themselves. Like the humans, they kept on going with a regimen of paracetamol and ibuprofen.

Thursday class was the worst – it dragged to twenty times its usual length because I was anticipating seeing Connor so much. Sidnee was also antsy; she'd invited Thomas to come and see her but he hadn't managed to confirm. I hoped for her sake that he'd come.

She checked her phone and flopped onto her bed. 'He's not coming.' Her voice wobbled.

'What?' I'd been too busy daydreaming about getting horizontal with Connor to pay attention.

'Thomas – he isn't coming.' Sidnee sighed. 'He's been hired to track down a feral werebear that attacked some kids. I know that's a valid reason not to come, but I was really hoping for a visitor.'

I went over to lay beside her on the narrow bed. 'I'm so sorry, Sid.'

She sniffed then squared her shoulders. 'It's okay. I guess I'll stay around here and see if I can get some more dirt on Petrovich Peril.'

At that moment, my own excitement seemed petty. 'I promise Connor and I will come back here and help.'

She gave me a wan smile. 'Don't you dare! One of us should be having a good time. Anyway, it's for the best because I'm still not sure if this thing with Thomas will work. It would be hard to always play second fiddle to his job, you know? Besides, I really don't have great luck with men.' She gave a small, helpless shrug.

'Thomas is a good one, Sidnee.'

'I think he is, but at this point I'm not sure what my judgement is worth.'

I cuddled her. 'Hey! You have great judgement. I've seen it time and time again. Chris was the outlier but you can trust Thomas. I've seen how he looks at you and how careful he was when he saved you from the otterman. He's good people – when he isn't hunting supernats. I bet it's killing him to let you down.'

'I suppose. But the whole thing with the MIB gave me pause.'

I blinked. 'What thing?' That was the first I'd heard of Thomas being involved with the MIB.

'Oh, I thought you knew.' She bit her bottom lip. 'I probably shouldn't have said anything. Anyway, he doesn't work for them anymore.' She gave me a playful shove and half-knocked me off the bed. 'Go on! You need to get ready. You don't have time to mope with me.' She swept her eyes up and down me critically. 'You need a transformation of the highest order.'

'Hey!' I objected, but she wasn't wrong. I was covered in mud from the obstacle course and I definitely needed a shower.

Sidnee's news had dampened my mood a little, but I was still nearly dancing with anticipation. Connor had already messaged that he was here in Sitka and he'd gotten us a place for the weekend. He was picking me up in an hour.

When Sidnee wasn't looking, I pulled out my phone and texted him. *Thomas can't come for Sidnee. Gunnar and Sigrid are run ragged but could you maybe see if Stan can come? And then make it happen? Helicopters? Private jets? Whatever you need to do? Please, Connor?*

I grabbed my stuff for the shower and went to clean up. By the time I was back, I had a response. *I hope helping you with that blowhard bear gets me major boyfriend points. He'll be a little late, but he's on his way.*

I suppressed a squeal of joy. It would be better for Stan to surprise Sidnee so, with an effort, I kept a lid on my happiness. *You are literally the best boyfriend in the whole world. I can't wait to see you! Xx*

60 minutes and counting, came the reply. They couldn't pass fast enough.

I impressed myself by showering, shaving my legs and doing my make up in only forty minutes; I really was a miracle worker. But as I was pulling on my black-leather boots, complete with stiletto heels, the shouting and screaming began.

And like all heroines in horror movies, I bolted *towards* the sound.

Chapter 16

The common room consisted of a couple of couches, tables, other seating, and a large TV and a whiteboard. Most of the recruits had already left for Commander's Weekend when I pelted in so it wasn't too busy – but I guessed it was busy enough for Petty.

Margi, Danny, George and Eben were in a maelstrom of flying chairs, couches, anything not attached to the floor, ducking and diving to try and avoid injury.

'Petrovich Peril, I command you to stop,' I said loudly. Hey, if it worked with Aoife, maybe it would work with Petty. I was proud of myself for the authoritative tone that snapped out; there wasn't even a tiny little stutter to betray the grip of fear around my heart. These guys were my friends and they could be injured if I didn't get the poltergeist to stop. Even though they were supernat, that could still hurt like a bitch. We were lucky that none of the human recruits were there.

Petty ignored my command and threw a chair in my direction. Sidnee grabbed my elbow and yanked me back. 'Don't step into the room,' she said urgently. 'It'll trap you, too.' She was clutching a bundle of what I assumed was sage. 'I stole some sage from the kitchens earlier. I knew it was only a matter of time before we'd need it,' she said grimly. 'Do you remember the prayer of St Michael the Archangel?'

I gave her a flat look. Of course I did.

'Right. You recite it while I cleanse the room.' She pulled out a lighter and held it to the bundle of silvered greenery in her hand, then blew on it until the sage was putting out white smoke. 'Now, Bunny,' she snapped.

I nodded and pulled up the prayer from my memory. I hadn't been raised religious but my mother, being who she was, had kept on good terms with the local Church of England diocese. Connor had written it down for me in his fifteen-page email but I already knew the prayer by heart.

I took a deep breath and chanted loudly, 'Saint Michael the Archangel, defend us in battle. Be our protection against the wickedness and snares of the devil; May God rebuke him, we humbly pray; And do thou, O Prince of the Heavenly Host, by the power of God, thrust into hell

Satan and all evil spirits who wander through the world for the ruin of souls. Amen.'

As I followed Sidnee as she moved around the edges of the room. I realised she was also chanting the prayer. When we reached the third corner the turbulence decreased. Sidnee was able to approach the recruits and bathe them in smoke as we recited the prayer one more time. The poltergeist gave up and fled, and the furniture fell to the ground with a resounding crash.

We all stared at each other. 'Hey,' I said into the stunned silence. 'You guys okay?'

'Holy smokes,' Margi uttered. 'That was scary as heck.'

'I've been better,' George agreed shakily. He had a cut on his forehead that looked nasty.

'I'm okay,' Danny said. He looked at George. 'You'd better shift or that will scar.'

'You keep watch?' George asked nervously.

We girls took point along the corridor whilst George stripped and shifted. A few minutes later Danny called out, 'You can come back in.'

George was pulling on his T-shirt. 'Oh,' said Margi with visible dismay. 'I thought we were going to see him in wolverine form! Why, colour me disappointed!'

George winked. 'I'll shift for you anytime, Margilene.' Then his smile faded and his face paled. He pointed at the whiteboard. 'Look.'

You're all going to die, the message said. It looked like it had been written by a shaky, uncertain hand; Petty must have written it before he'd become immersed in his fury. For whatever reason, it seemed like he was fixating on us supernats.

Boy, had he picked the wrong group to bully.

Chapter 17

Seeing Connor almost took my breath away. He was leaning on a small white truck; it was a little beat up, and I had no idea where it had come from. His hair was in its usual tousled state and I knew he'd been running his hands through it. Maybe he was a little nervous to see me after so long apart.

Connor had more money than anyone I knew – including my parents – yet he was dressed in his simple brown work boots, jeans and a flannel shirt. And because he knew it melted me; his flannel shirt was rolled up to display his powerful forearms.

I moved without conscious thought – and far too fast – as I zipped with accidental vampire speed right into his arms. I dropped my bag and flung myself at him like he was the oxygen I needed. I wrapped my legs tightly around his waist, lowered my lips to his and lost myself in the taste and smell of Connor, my home.

The bond between us gave an almighty *zing*, and the clawing anxiety that had been growling in my stomach eased for the first time in weeks. *Home.* Such a yummy home. The scent of sandalwood, bergamot and vanilla filled my nostrils. He smelled *divine.*

When Jones yelled cheekily at us to 'get a room', I reddened and my hands stilled on the buttons of Connor's shirt. I'd undone all but one of them, displaying his chest for me – and everyone else – to admire. I hadn't been thinking of anything but getting that man inside me, *now,* and I'd completely forgotten where we were. His heaving chest and dark eyes said the same.

I reluctantly let him go and slid down to place my feet back on the ground. We both took several gulping breaths. If Jones hadn't said anything, we would totally have fucked on the hood of his truck. Eep.

Without a hint of self-consciousness, Connor undid the last button of his shirt because it was easier than doing them all back up again. He put his hand in the small of my back, led me to the passenger side of the truck and opened the door. As I slid in, he slung my bag into the boot. We still hadn't spoken a single word, but sometimes words weren't necessary.

Connor climbed into the driver's side and looked at me with a gaze that was still scorching. 'Hey,' I said.

A smile curved his lips. 'Hey, Bunny. It's damn good to see you.'

I grinned. 'You too. I've never been happier to see anyone in my whole life.'

He reached out, laced his fingers through mine and closed his eyes. 'What you do to me,' he murmured. He took another deep breath and opened his eyes, then turned the key in the ignition and we motored off. I didn't know where we were going and truthfully I didn't care. All I wanted was a couple of days away from the academy and that damned poltergeist.

Seeing Connor was a dream come true, but it also gave me a wave of longing for Portlock. I missed Fluffy and Shadow, and I missed Gunnar and Sigrid. I even missed Stan. I brightened at the thought that hopefully I'd get to see him before he left. He wasn't Fluffy or Shadow, but he would definitely be better than nothing.

The truck hit a rut in the road and we bounced around in the cab for about five minutes afterwards. 'I like the vehicle,' I said a little sarcastically. 'Great suspension.'

Connor laughed. 'I hear you. It turns out it's hard to find a rental on the island. I was told this was the last one and it was, quote, "a beater with a heater".'

It was certainly that: it was a basic model with a manual and no extras. You had to roll down the windows with the little arm thingy – not that you needed to because it was cold outside. I was glad it wasn't raining since my bag was in the back and it had no cover.

We were wedged into the cab together with barely room for Connor to change gear. The tight confines totally nixed my idea of having truck sex; I'd have to wait for an actual bed – heck, a sofa would do.

Connor turned left on the highway out of town, drove less than a mile and pulled into a petrol station. We didn't fill up; instead he drove through to the back where there was a brewery. 'Are we going to dinner?' I asked, and my stomach growled a little. I could always eat.

'We sure are, but I thought you'd like to see your surprise first.'

I beamed and bounced on the small seat. I loved surprises! 'You know me. I can't wait!'

He smiled indulgently and squeezed my hand. 'I do know you. You're going to love it.' I hoped so. My expectations were high and I expected good things of Connor Mackenzie.

At the back of the brewery there was a small apartment building where he parked up. 'This is where we're staying. All of these apartments are Airbnbs,' he explained.

He came around to open my door and help me out then picked up my bag and ushered me towards a ground-floor apartment – and hopefully my surprise.

Chapter 18

Connor knocked on our apartment door, which made me frown. Why was he knocking? Then he immediately punched in the door code and opened the door without waiting for a response. Oh-kay.

He tossed my bag on a chair whilst I looked around. It was a fair-sized studio apartment with a small bathroom in the back. It reminded me of my old flat in London, though it was bigger, cleaner and had nicer furnishing.

I couldn't see any packages or anything. Hmm... Where was my surprise? Then the door to the bathroom, which hadn't been fully closed, flew open and Fluffy and Shadow came bounding towards me.

'Oh!' My eyes filled with tears as I squatted down to greet the most wonderful surprise ever. My complicated four-legged friends engulfed me with their exuberant greetings and love – plus an extra side of spit from Fluffy, who must have just had a drink. Lovely. Let's hope it hadn't been a drink from the toilet.

'I missed both of you so much!' I tried to stroke them both at the same time. Shadow jumped on my shoulder and buried his purring face under my hair and into my neck. I grabbed the heavy kitten and snuggled him until he squirmed. Fluffy waited patiently for his turn, sitting on his haunches with his head cocked. His tail hadn't stopped wagging since he'd seen me. Once Shadow jumped down, he walked over calmly and put his head in my hands. I gave him several full body cuddles as I murmured how happy I was to see him.

'I can't believe you brought them to me!' I said to Connor after the love fest was over. 'How did you pull that off?'

'Well, I chartered a plane – for Shadow, mainly – so that was easy. It was a little harder with the Airbnb, but I convinced them it would be fine.'

There was something in his tone that told me there was more to that story 'How?' I pressed. I continued to scruff Fluffy's ears and caress Shadow as he rubbed against me.

'In the end I rented all of the apartments so no other guests would mind about the animals,' Connor said matter of factly. 'Prime season is over and they had all of these vacancies...' He trailed off as I leapt up and threw my arms around his neck. I started to kiss him again as we fell back on the bed.

A whine from Fluffy slowed us down and Connor chuckled. 'Fluffy has his own room with Shadow, but first we're going out to dinner like I promised.' He sat up and looked at Fluffy. 'You promised you'd come too, so you'd better change,' he said to my dog.

Fluffy whined and dropped his head. 'I'd love to see you, Reggie,' I said softly. 'But if you want to stay Fluffy for a bit longer, that's okay with me, too.'

He lowered his head and gave another low whine, but then he shifted and Reggie was standing in his place in his black jeans and black jacket. 'Can I have a hug?' I asked lightly. 'The academy has me attention starved.'

Reggie stepped into my arms and rested his head on my shoulder. A fierce wave of protectiveness rose up in me; I wanted nothing more than to see this lad happy and free, but it was very much a work in progress. Something about his situation reminded me of Lieutenant Fischer's lecture; Reggie wasn't quite in a Stockholm Syndrome situation, but he was in something similar.

He was institutionalised into being Fluffy so being Reggie was hard and scary. When he was Fluffy, he lost a lot of his human cerebral capabilities; he became a smart dog, but a *dog*, nonetheless, ruled by instinct rather than by making conscious choices. For Reggie, being Fluffy was the easier option.

'I'll come to dinner,' he said shyly. 'But then I can go back to being Fluffy, okay? I like being Fluffy.'

I nodded sadly. I loved him as Fluffy, too, but that wasn't who he truly was. It was going to be a long road to get him back to wanting to be human again. I wondered if we could find him a psychologist in Portlock; there had to be one.

Connor consulted his watch. 'We should go,' he said.

Reggie, with his black clothing, skinny build and shy, quiet demeanour, could pass as a local teenager as long as he didn't talk. His London accent would instantly give him away as being different. Not that I cared about that – I was different, too.

It was a tight squeeze with all of us in the truck. Changing gears was interesting, since the gear shift was between my legs. If Connor and I had been alone, it would have been a titillating experience.

Reggie was staring out of the window, his shoulders hunched. He was way out of his comfort zone. I gave his hand a reassuring squeeze and he half-smiled in response.

Thankfully it was only a couple of miles to the restaurant. I hadn't seen much of Sitka so I enjoyed the drive, short though it was. After flying in, Sidnee and I had been driven over the bridge and straight to the academy, so we'd only seen the place from that short bus ride and our quick run through town looking for totem poles. It was truly beautiful: wooded, historic, and green, even at the end of autumn.

The restaurant was on the main floor of the historic Sitka Hotel. When we were ushered in and seated, Reggie squirmed, kept his eyes averted and slouched as low as he could in his seat. He was painfully shy and I wondered if he'd been like that before he'd been turned into a werewolf. He appeared confident when he was Fluffy, but he'd told me he was barely aware of his human self when he was a dog. That was different from his life as a werewolf, where he was fully aware of both selves, and it was why it was so damaging for him to be stuck as a dog rather than a werewolf. It was another tally mark against Mum.

The waiter came and took our drinks orders, passed out food menus and gave us some water. Reggie looked nervous. 'What's wrong?' I asked softly.

'I haven't eaten as a human in a long while. What if I can't remember how to use a knife and fork?'

I thought back. The day we'd broken the curse we'd had a small party and though Reggie had helped us prepare the food, he hadn't eaten. He'd helped us clean up, had a shower then gone back to being Fluffy.

Connor's eyes were kind and he nodded in understanding. He squeezed Reggie gently on the shoulder. 'We'll help. Don't worry.'

'You'll remember,' I assured him. 'It's probably like riding a bike. You'll do great.'

'I'll try. Thanks, guys.'

I handed him the basket of bread on the table. 'Why don't we start with something with no knives and forks? Take a roll and take a small bite. We'll practise together.' Connor and I demonstrated.

Reggie watched us carefully then copied us. We all ate some bread, then he tackled the glass of water. He lifted it to his lips and took a small sip. His shoulders relaxed and his smile widened as he managed that small task without incident. 'Thanks,' he said softly. 'I was scared I'd choke or make a mess, but it's not so different.'

This time I reached out and took his hand. 'Anxiety is normal but remember that we're always here for you. You can be Reggie any time you wish.'

He smiled wanly at me. 'Fluffy is easier and I'm useful as Fluffy. I like being useful. I'm ... well, as Reggie I'm nothing. I'm not even a werewolf anymore.'

'You're not nothing,' I said firmly. 'None of us are nothing. Every human and supernat on this planet deserves to be treated as something, *someone*. If anyone ever makes you feel less, you tell me or Connor and we'll beat them into a bloody pulp for you.'

Reggie smiled again. 'Thanks.'

'Bunny!' I heard a familiar voice and turned in time to see Sidnee flying towards me with Stan trailing in her wake. I stood up in time to get an armful of my best friend. 'You sneak!' she teased. 'You got Stan to visit!'

I grinned. 'I asked and he was more than willing to come. And Connor sorted out the flights and stuff.'

'Mackenzie.' Stan gave Connor a neutral nod.

'Ahmaogak.' Connor nodded back, expression also carefully neutral. Stan sat opposite him and the two men held eye contact for entirely too long.

Sidnee huffed. 'Can you two just be Stan and Connor for one damned dinner? Leave your titles and politics at the door?'

Connor looked amused. 'Yes, ma'am.'

Stan looked at him. 'She's small but feisty. Frankly, I've always found it easier to do what she says.'

'He's not wrong,' I agreed.

Reggie had a small smile on his face, which was worth all the silly bickering in the world. Stan patted him on the back in greeting; I'd seen Stan push people over with that gesture but he didn't even sway Reggie's frame.

'Thank you,' I mouthed and Stan winked back at me.

'So.' Stan sat back and helped himself to some bread. 'Have you both been having a nice holiday?'

'Holiday?' Sidnee screeched. 'I'll give you a holiday!' She swatted him on the arm.

Now *this* was home.

Chapter 19

Dinner went smoothly. I thought that Reggie was a little more comfortable in his skin by the end of it, but when we returned to the truck he looked around to check no one was looking and instantly shifted back into Fluffy. I sighed; it was a work in progress. I loved my dog but he was a person too, and I ached that he liked being a dog more than being himself – but everyone had the right to be what they wanted to be.

'It'll take time,' Stan murmured. 'I've seen shifters who lost themselves to their animal forms come back to human, but you gotta be patient. Don't push too much. Just be there for him.'

'Always.' I sighed.

'You're a good person.' He gave me a one-armed hug. 'I can't stay too long. Sidnee and I are going to have a movie night and then I'm taking her out tomorrow for breakfast.

After that, I'm flying back – I've got a meeting I can't be late for.'

'So this is goodbye?' I felt unexpectedly emotional. Man, this homesickness was doing a number on me. I couldn't *wait* to get back to Portlock in a couple of weeks, even if it would be to my favourite situation: situation normal, all fucked up.

'For now.' He flashed me one of his exuberant, cheeky grins. 'Hey, what's a bunny's favourite mode of transport?'

I groaned.

'A hareplane!'

I groaned even louder, making Stan laugh. 'I'll be seeing you, Bunny.'

'See you, Stan. Thanks for coming. It means the world to Sidnee and to me.'

A hint of wistfulness filled his gaze as he looked at me. 'Anytime.'

I broke the awkward moment by giving Sidnee a big hug goodbye. 'You're the best,' she whispered.

'Back at you, lady. Have a fun night.'

They motored off in a truck that looked a darned sight better than the monstrosity Connor and I were riding in.

'How did you do it?'

'Do what?'

'Get him here in...' I checked my phone for the time. 'Four hours?'

He gave a casual shrug and unlocked my door. 'I know a guy.'

'Does he have a portal?'

Connor laughed. 'No, he has a very nice helicopter.'

I slid into the cab next to Fluffy and scratched his ears. He leaned into me and I put my arm around him as Connor drove us back to the Airbnb.

When we arrived, Connor looked at Fluffy. 'You still haven't told her,' he said softly. A beat later, Fluffy became Reggie.

'Told me what?' I asked, putting my arm back around my young friend.

He let out a breath. 'Connor – well, I agreed, but the academy reached out to the Nomo's office to have you and me do a K-9 presentation. It's a three-day thing, but only for an hour each class.' Reggie squirmed and looked at me hopefully. 'If you want to, that is.'

I beamed at him. 'Absolutely! It'll be so much fun. We'll blow them away!'

Reggie smiled. 'I'll be the best K-9 they've ever seen.' I was positive that he would be. As Fluffy he was formidable, and he knew it. I was determined that one day he would know his worth as a human, too.

Reggie said a quiet goodnight then went to his and Shadow's room next door. I was pleased that at least he walked out as a human.

As Connor and I went into our room, I wondered what I would do with three hours of K-9 class. I had no training and no teaching experience. Usually we winged it when we were working and used Fluffy's intelligence to get us through by the seat of our pants. I knew from the movies that a lot of highly trained dogs were taught commands in German but neither Fluffy nor I spoke a lick of German. I'd studied French and Latin; French had been useful when I vacationed in southern France in my youth, but no one *spoke* Latin.

Well, this K-9 and handler spoke English, so that would have to do.

'Penny for your thoughts?' Connor asked me.

'I'm thinking about the K-9 classes,' I admitted. 'Obviously Fluffy will do anything I ask of him, but I don't know anything about being a proper K-9 handler. I'm going to have to spend some of our time together doing research if we want to pull this off.'

Connor nodded. 'I know, but I think it'll be worth it. Reggie's self-confidence is so low, I thought this might bring him out of his shell a little, help him see his own worth. Then we can try and apply Fluffy's confidence to Reggie.'

'It's a great idea.' I kissed him. 'And so thoughtful of you. Have I told you how much I love how much you care for my...' I trailed off: 'dog' wasn't quite the right word.

'I know what you mean. Anyway, I'm not throwing you in the deep end without giving you some tools to kick ass with.'

'I do like kicking ass,' I said brightly. 'What tools have you got for me?'

'A training manual. With your memory, you'll have it down before you're put on the spot.'

I felt some relief at that. I had a superdog that no one knew was human under the fur, and I knew he'd do everything perfectly; frankly, I was the weakest link here. But I did have an excellent memory and the ability to absorb a book in record time. I could do this.

I slid Connor a sidelong glance. I suspected that Fluffy's wasn't the only confidence he was trying to bolster. He took a kettle out of his bag, filled it with water and started to make me an honest-to-goodness cup of tea. 'You're making me tea,' I said dumbly.

He gave me his lopsided grin. 'I'd give you the world if I could, but tea will have to do.'

I moved towards him and spoke some words I never *ever* thought I'd hear myself say. 'Fuck the tea.'

We stared at each other for a long moment then lunged. Without knowing quite how we got there, we were soon tangled on the bed and our clothes were disappearing as if by magic.

I wrapped myself in Connor and all my worries fled.

Chapter 20

When my alarm woke me at dawn after maybe an hour of sleep, my worries came flooding back. Connor was still asleep; it was daytime and he was on vampire time like I should have been, but I had to stay on academy time or going back would be a bitch. It would be jet lag times a million – no thank you.

I had to stay awake so I decided to use the time to creepily watch my boyfriend sleep then maybe read the manual he'd brought me. First, though, I checked on my animals. Fluffy wanted out. For the life of me I didn't know why he didn't shift and use the facilities, but I guessed his need to be Fluffy outweighed his discomfort at having to wait to be let out to go to the toilet. We had a long way to go. I comforted myself with Stan's words: it would take time, but it would be possible for him to acclimatise to a human life again.

Shadow rubbed my legs, purred, then looked pointedly at his empty dishes. I had no idea what food Connor had brought so I checked the small fridge. There was a bag of the raw food mix I kept for Shadow at home; Connor must have grabbed some from the freezer. I'd had the vet and the internet help me come up with a diet for a lynx. It was a mess to make because I had to grind several types of meat together with vitamins and minerals, but it was worth it to have a healthy kitten.

Since I didn't want to disturb Connor, I sat down at the tiny kitchen table in Fluffy and Shadow's room to read the manual. I started with the section *Tracking with a K-9* because it was something we did a lot at work and I was comfortable with it. The other two topics were *Search and Rescue* and *Drug Detecting*. I shivered as I thought about the Savik brothers on our first search and rescue. We'd retrieved bodies, not living men – but at least we'd found them.

Drug Detecting also made me wince. Technically, our fisheye case was still open. We knew who had been dealing in town, but the case had become much more involved when an army general had shown up and we became aware that Portlock had been chosen as a black government site for experimenting on supernats. The damned black-ops soldiers were still on the loose, and I feared they were using fisheye and other drugs in other paranormal towns. Taking them down was still very much on my to-do list.

The textbook was comprehensive, and I realised that Gunnar already knew all this stuff because he'd had Killer, a real trained K-9. Although Fluffy had never been formally trained, it was clear that Gunnar had been quietly teaching him when we went out on calls, so a lot of the information wasn't as new as I'd feared it would be.

By the time I'd finished reading, I was feeling a lot more optimistic. We could absolutely do this – or at least Fluffy could and I could act as if I knew what I was doing. Fake it till you make it.

I checked the clock: 5pm. I hurriedly looked up the time for sunset on my phone: 6.20pm. I had a little time to kill, time to sneak back into our apartment and get cleaned up. I was in the mood for a long, luxurious shower.

I was rinsing my hair and indulging in the warm water when a hand snaked in and touched my shoulder. My eyes were closed so I squealed and jumped, but the hand was followed by a very warm and naked man whom I instantly recognised.

'I was trying to let you sleep,' I said as I turned to face him. It was a very small shower. It would have been hard to pick up the soap if you dropped it, even if you were alone; it would have been impossible if you were sharing the minuscule unit with another person.

'I can sleep at home. Right now you're here, warm and wet in the shower and smelling of...' he checked the shampoo bottle '...lavender and vanilla. How could I resist?'

'If you want more than your hair washed, we'll have to get out of this tiny shower. There is zero room to manoeuvre,' I said with a flirty lilt in my voice.

'You think so, do you?' Connor gave a confident smirk.

I kissed him quickly. 'I know so!' Then I put my hands out and touched all three walls of the shower and the curtain. 'See? No room for shenanigans.'

Connor's eyes twinkled. In a single move, he lifted me up against the shower wall. 'Hey! That's cold!' I objected.

He grinned. 'I've got a few ideas on how to warm you up.'

I shivered – and not because of the cold plastic tiles against my wet skin. 'Oh, it's like that is it?' I wrapped my legs around him and leaned down to kiss him again.

It turned out that the small shower was big enough to get really dirty in.

When Connor dropped me off at the end of the Commander's Weekend, I was exhausted. Between enjoying him and practising with Fluffy for our demonstrations, I'd had very little sleep – though I wasn't complaining in the slightest. It was exactly the pick-me-up I'd needed, even if I couldn't stop yawning.

I'd pushed the poltergeist's ominous message to the back of my mind. I hadn't mentioned the threat to Connor because he had a tendency to overreact to death threats to my person; also, it was hard to get worked up about Petty's message. Something about the whole thing felt *off*, but for the life of me I couldn't put my finger on what. However, when we drove up the academy, it all came rushing back. It was time for me to roll up my sleeves and get stuck in.

I kissed Connor, ruffled Fluffy's ears and collected my bag. 'See you,' Connor said simply.

I smiled. 'See you.' He would be on the island a little longer to look after Fluffy until it was time for his academy K-9 debut, so this wasn't goodbye. I'd get to see him again soon, even if it was for only a handful of precious seconds as he dropped off and picked up Fluffy. I'd do my damnedest to make sure we had some time for fraternisation.

I waved them goodbye and turned back to the academy with a bounce in my step. I was going to solve Petty's mystery if it was the last thing I did.

Chapter 21

Sidnee was excited to see me. 'How was it?' she asked, bouncing on the bed. I smirked. She threw a pillow at my head. 'That's not what I meant!' She grinned. 'Though I'm sure that part was good because you look exhausted. I meant finding out about you and Fluffy teaching the classes.'

'You knew?'

'Of course, I knew! Connor needed me to get in touch with Sergeant Marks and arrange it.' She cackled a shade maliciously. 'I cannot *wait* to see Thorsen's face when he realises he has to take a class from you!'

I hadn't thought of that. I was almost hopeful that he would try to disrupt my lessons. Would I get away with ordering him to run laps if he disrespected me?

'Did anything happen while I was gone?' I asked. 'Any – you know...' I fluttered my fingers '...activity?' I looked around as though I could see the poltergeist.

'No, nothing as far as I know. It's been quiet since we did the prayer and the cleansing.'

'Were many people still around?'

She shook her head. 'No, only a handful of us recruits with nothing else to do.'

I sat cross-legged on her bed and faced her. 'So, what *did* you do? After Stan dropped you back, I mean.'

The bouncing resumed. 'Do you know what? It was great. I slept in, caught up on the reading for next week and watched a lot of stupid cat videos on my phone.' She giggled. 'It was actually a real winner of a weekend. And I ventured out to see Sitka, too. I bet I saw more of it then you did.' She waggled her eyebrows.

I laughed. 'I'm sure you did. All my spare time was spent preparing to do those three K-9 classes.'

She did the eyebrow thing again. 'Not all of your spare time, I'm sure.' She laughed, then sobered. 'I'm not worried about the class. Fluffy knows what he's doing, and you two have worked together for months. You've got this.'

I nodded. 'I feel better about it now, but that doesn't change the fact that I don't have any formal training. I don't even know the terms real K-9 handlers use, and neither Fluffy nor I speak German.'

'German?' She shot me a perplexed glance.

'Yeah, apparently it's a thing. But it doesn't matter – we'll be doing this in English.'

'English is good. I doubt a single person here speaks German.'

'I know, but it's supposed to be a command language for a lot of K-9s.'

She shoved my shoulder. 'Don't fret! You'll be fine.'

'Thanks.' I shot her a grateful smile.

It was almost time for lights-out and I was really excited about having some actual honest-to-goodness sleep. I put my things away and got ready for bed. I thought I'd fall asleep instantly, but my first K-9 demonstration was the next day and it was playing on my mind. I spent a lot of time rehearsing what I would say, and by the time I finally fell asleep it was already into the witching hours.

I slept fitfully and kept waking up to check the time. It sucked, and I knew I'd struggle in the morning, but my stupid brain would not shush.

When the alarm went off, I got up sluggishly, dressed by rote and followed Sidnee to PT. I was so exhausted that I almost didn't make it through the physical training, mats and the obstacle course. I yawned my way through breakfast, too.

The only thing going for me was that Connor would arrive after breakfast with Fluffy, but even so I was a bundle of nerves. I looked around the cafeteria at my fellow recruits and wondered if they'd accept me teaching them or if they'd laugh me out of the academy. Then I squared my shoulders. I was a Nomo officer and a K-9 handler. I was not going to embarrass Gunnar *or* Fluffy, and I was absolutely going to smash this. They would respect my authority. I snickered in my head as I heard *South Park* in my head. They *would* respect my authority – what little shred of it I had.

Besides, I could absolutely depend on Thorsen to be a twat and that would give me the opportunity to put him down – hard. I was *really* looking forward to that. There had been a time in my life when I'd toed the line and kept my head down, trying my darndest to please my parents and so many other people, but I'd kissed that attitude goodbye the day I'd kissed Franklin, my sire. Portlock had been the making of me; maybe Sitka could be the making of Thorsen if he pulled his head out of his arse long enough to actually *learn.*

As I got up to leave, Sidnee grabbed my arm and whispered an encouraging, 'You got this.' As always, I had at least one person on my side.

I put my tray away, then went to meet Connor and collect Fluffy. Connor was leaning against his beat-up truck in front of the main doors looking like my own personal wet dream. Next to him, Fluffy was ready to rock and roll in his Nomo vest. He looked freshly brushed and sharp. Nice.

'Thank you for doing this,' I said to Connor for the hundredth time. 'I know it's keeping you from home and work.'

'Exactly.' He grinned. 'Any excuse.' He shot me a wink before pulling me in for a slow kiss that got every cell in my body dancing the cha-cha-cha. 'It's worth it for that,' he breathed huskily, then released me and gave me a light swat on the bottom. 'Now, go get 'em, tiger.'

I blew him another kiss, grabbed Fluffy's lead and sauntered inside as if I actually knew what I was doing. I walked to the doors with my head held high; I was ready to educate, to show these guys and gals what a difference a good police dog could make.

I made my way to the front of the class with Fluffy trotting to heel, then gave him the hand signal to sit. He sat immediately and watched me intently, ready for his next instruction. I turned to take in the class, which had fallen totally silent.

All eyes were on me, most of them surprised, though Thorsen and his gang were looking at me with total disbelief. I could almost hear 'you gotta be kidding me!' rolling around inside their heads.

Fluffy remained sitting, his eyes fixed on me, a perfect K-9 specimen. Marks came to the front of the class and everyone switched their attention to him. 'We're pleased to have a K-9 handler here today to demonstrate some of their skills and abilities. This is one of your fellow recruits, Elizabeth "Bunny" Barrington from Nanwalek...'

I blinked a bit at hearing Nanwalek and not Portlock, but we'd agreed beforehand that if anyone asked, Sidnee and I couldn't say we were from a place that the peds *knew* was a notorious ghost town. Nanwalek was a native village of around three hundred people, and it was unlikely anyone here would know it. Sidnee was claiming to be from Seldovia, another village on the Kenai Peninsula. Marks had checked beforehand to make sure none of the other recruits were from our fake villages; this clearly wasn't his first rodeo.

I turned back to him as he gestured at my German Shepherd. 'And this is her K-9, Fluffy,' he said.

There were a few titters in the crowd at Fluffy's name and a full-on snort of derision from Thorsen. Marks fixed him with a hard look and he settled down. I ignored them all. Once they'd seen what Fluffy could do, they wouldn't give a fuck about his name. I plastered on my best fake smile.

Marks continued, 'Barrington is going to do demos over the next three days. I'll have her introduce what those will be.' He turned expectantly to me.

'Thank you, sir.' I swallowed. 'Erm...' My throat felt tight: a coughing fit was not what I needed right now. I breathed deeply. 'Right. So, the three classes we'll perform will be tracking, search and rescue, and drug identification. We'll start with tracking. I've asked Sergeant Marks to bury three items for this demonstration, and I don't have any idea where they are. We'll start out back by the obstacle course, so if everyone will follow me?'

I hated that it came out as a question rather than an order, but everyone rose dutifully to their feet and followed me – even Thorsen and his crew.

Maybe I *could* do this after all.

Chapter 22

Once we were outside, I had my fellow recruits gather in a spot where it was clear that none of the items had been buried. I raised my voice. 'Fluffy has tracked several things for us in real-life cases. We've worked together to locate some missing hikers, found evidence, and tracked down suspected perpetrators. Tracking with a K-9 unit can be a huge advantage, especially in time-sensitive cases.'

I leaned down, unhooked Fluffy's lead and gave him a quick ruffle for confidence, then turned back to the assembled recruits. 'I've had Sergeant Marks bury three items – a piece of clothing, a raw chicken leg and a small bag containing marijuana.'

One of Thorsen's group, Frederick Miller, raised his hand, his expression pugnacious. I braced myself but chose to face his heckling head on. 'Yes?' I called on him.

'Marijuana is perfectly legal in Alaska,' he sneered. 'Or, being a foreigner, didn't you know that?'

Sergeant Marks turned around and looked like he was going to say something but I put up a hand. I didn't need him to intercede on my behalf; I needed to show everyone, including myself, that I could handle this.

I gave Frederick a flat look. 'It's only for demonstration purposes. Besides, I didn't think you'd appreciate me borrowing your cocaine.' I gave him a saucy wink and the class burst into laughter. Miller turned a pleasing shade of red.

Visibly dismissing him, I turned back to the class. 'Which item should we find first?' I asked the others.

Jones raised his hand. 'The chicken leg?' he asked timidly.

'Absolutely. The chicken will be easy for a dog to find since they have incredible noses, plus food is necessary for us all. It's useful to know that your dog can always find you sustenance, no matter where you are.' Despite myself, my mind wandered to surviving beyond the barrier.

I cleared my throat again and forced my brain to focus, then pulled out three plastic bags from my backpack. 'Scent tracking is different from other kinds. We want to start with showing the dog what scent he is looking for,' I explained.

I held the bag with a piece of raw chicken in it out to Fluffy and gave him the verbal command 'smell'. He obeyed although, truth be told, if I'd said 'headless chicken' he'd still have found it. But this was a class and I wanted to do it properly. 'Seek,' I ordered.

Fluffy turned and, nose down, began searching for the chicken leg. He snuffled this way and that along the earth, wandering around in a circle. It was immediately clear when he caught the scent because he froze, lifted one of his forepaws and looked in the direction he thought the object was. 'This stance is called pointing,' I explained. 'He's showing us where he wants to go. To confirm his instructions, I'll tell him again. Fluffy, seek.'

Obediently, Fluffy's nose shot down to the ground again and he snuffled forward to an area where it had been disturbed. He stood over it, turned to me and whined. 'Fluffy, retrieve,' I commanded.

He began digging; the chicken hadn't been buried too deeply and in a moment he'd uncovered it. He turned, barked at me, then sat next to his prize looking chuffed.

I confirmed that he had indeed found the chicken and patted him on the head. 'Good boy.' I turned to the class. 'Dinner, anyone?' I joked. There was a gratifying array of chuckles.

'You'll note,' I said, 'that Fluffy has found the chicken but he hasn't picked it up, mouthed it or eaten it.' There were a few appreciative nods, no doubt from the recruits who knew how much willpower and training it took for a dog not to devour food on the spot. 'Anyone else want to choose what comes next?'

'Yeah, the marijuana,' one of Thorsen's sidekicks said, eyes still flashing with challenge.

I sighed inwardly but forced my face into a pleasant expression, picked up the scent bag for Fluffy and repeated the process. Marijuana had a strong scent so it was easy for a dog to locate. Fluffy had his nose to the ground in a moment and his stance set to pointing only a few sniffs later. I repeated the command to seek and he hastened forward. It wasn't a large area to search and in moments he'd uncovered the bag.

This time the recruits seemed a little more impressed. Everyone could appreciate how handy it was for your dog to be able to locate contraband, especially with such lightning-fast precision.

'Good boy,' I praised Fluffy again and passed Marks the baggie of weed. He pocketed it, and I resisted the urge to joke about him making me some special brownies.

The last item to be found was an old shirt that I'd worn for a day during Commander's Weekend. My scent on it was strong and I let Fluffy sniff a scrap of it. It had been hidden well, away from the immediate area around the side of the building, yet Fluffy shot to it with no effort.

I praised him calmly, but inwardly I was jumping up and down and cheering. He had totally smashed it and I was prouder than a mum when their child performed their first nativity play. Keeping a handle on my exuberance, I turned back to my audience. 'Any questions?'

'How do you teach them to do that?' a recruit asked.

'I'm not an expert on teaching handling,' I admitted, feeling an utter fraud. But I'd seen Gunnar train Fluffy back in the days when he'd thought Fluffy was a dog, so I did have some knowledge. 'But it's basically the same way the academy trains us – with a shit tonne of time, effort, treats and repetition.' There were some appreciative titters.

'How old is Fluffy?' someone else asked.

Since I couldn't say he was a nineteen-year-old former werewolf, I made up a number on the fly. 'He's five.'

'Has he brought down any perps?'

I nodded proudly. 'Oh yes. He's stopped several crimes.'

I was nervous that someone would ask something I couldn't answer and I stifled the urge to end question time. Another hand was raised. 'You used hand signals and vocal commands. Why is that?'

'Sometimes your dog will be working in a noisy environment and he'll still need to correctly interpret your commands. Similarly, there'll be occasions when stealth is required. Silent signals are a lot better when you're tracking a perp.'

'Has he ever located a dead body?'

I thought of the Savik brothers; both had been dead and Fluffy had helped find them. 'Yes. Yes he has.' That took the happy atmosphere down a notch or two, but it also felt right to end the session on a sombre note. We weren't out there to play with a dog, we were there to talk about a K-9 unit and its benefits.

It was starting to rain but luckily my hour was up. I dismissed the students and they jogged back inside. Marks turned to me. 'Great job,' he said, giving me a nod. 'You'll hand the dog off now to Mackenzie?'

'Yes, sir.'

'Good.' He nodded stiffly and marched off.

Fluffy and I went to the car park. By now the rain was falling even harder but suddenly I didn't care because

Connor was standing waiting for me. His dark hair was dripping but that didn't stop a slow, sensual smile curving those delicious lips. 'How did it go?' he asked.

I wanted to lick those raindrops right off him. All of them. It would be a long job, like painting the Forth Bridge, but I was totally up for it. 'We nailed it,' I managed to say, but it came out the wrong side of breathless.

His smile widened. 'Of course you did.' He moved closer. 'I didn't doubt you for a second. Either of you.' The space between us closed further until our bodies were pressed together. His left hand slid around my back as he pulled me into him.

I looked up at him as water poured down us both. 'Thank you,' I said, though my mind was blank and I had no idea what I was thanking him for.

He cupped my face gently. 'You're welcome,' he murmured, and then we were kissing. The warmth of him was a sharp contrast to the cold around me. The rain was buffeting us but I couldn't have given fewer fucks; all I felt was him, the press of his tongue against mine, the slide of his hand that was grasping my ass, pulling me to him as if he could make us one, here and now. I was on board with that plan. The scent of him swirled around me and the jolt between us was so strong that I gasped into his mouth.

Fluffy barked loudly and repeatedly. Connor pulled back and rested his forehead against mine. 'Good thing the dog's still got his head,' he groaned. 'I've all but lost mine.'

I rubbed against his denim trousers. 'I don't know – I think I've found one of them.'

He groaned more loudly. 'Witch,' he accused teasingly.

'Apparently so,' I said wryly. I sighed and looked at him with real longing. 'I've got to go. I've got class.'

'Education is important,' Connor agreed gravely. 'You should definitely go.' He leaned forward and gave me a final chaste swipe of his lips. 'Go and learn. Now. Or I'll drag you away to teach you something else.'

'Promises, promises,' I shot back. I was tempted to stay with him but I also had an annoying sense of duty. Gunnar had sent me to the academy to learn; he was killing himself to hold Portlock without Sidnee and me to help him, and here was I enjoying smouldering kisses in the rain.

I stepped away from Connor with a jerk as if I was pulling myself away from a magnet. 'Soon,' I blurted, though again I didn't know what I was promising.

'Soon,' he agreed. 'Go, Bunny, before I don't let you leave.'

I wanted to sass that I was a strong independent woman and he couldn't stop me from doing *anything,* but my knees were weak and my vocabulary had been reduced to incomprehensible noises that would surely only encourage him. I staggered back a few more spaces and the tension left his shoulders. He opened the door to the truck and Fluffy jumped up. Connor slid in after him, then they both watched me until I'd made it back inside the building. I sent them a finger wave and turned away.

I crept into the back of the classroom and settled on a chair at the back. The wind rattled the windows as I took my seat; I guessed it was a good thing I'd come in, out of the storm.

Sidnee shot me a wide-eyed look. 'What happened to you?' she mouthed.

'Rain,' I muttered.

She sniggered. 'Uh-huh...'

Try as I might, I couldn't focus on anything but replaying that kiss over and over again. The thing between Connor and I was truly fire. Every now and again I tried to drag my attention back to Fischer's lecture, but my thoughts kept bouncing between the kiss, my demonstration the next day and the poltergeist problem.

It sucked not having a tonne of free time to investigate Petty's situation. Part of me toyed with involving Sergeant Marks because he'd have access to old records and the like, but if Petty's issue was an internal one then the staff were the main suspects. Recruits came and went; if Petty was trying to shine a light on a problem here, surely it related to someone who worked here. Ugh. This was all so frustrating.

Sidnee poked me in the ribs. 'What?' I demanded.

Lieutenant Fischer cleared his throat. Crap on a stick. I looked up at him. 'Can you answer the question, Barrington?'

Bugger. I could feel a blush trying to rise but my floppy heart wasn't pushing enough blood for that. 'Can you repeat it?'

With narrowed eyes and a hint of impatience he said, 'What is the leading cause of death in cold-water immersion?'

I knew this. I leaned into my memory for the recall. 'Umm, cold-shock response.'

'Correct. What is that exactly?' he pressed.

'Um... It's a physiological response that includes gasping for air, uncontrollable rapid breathing that can lead to drowning, increased heart rate, peripheral vasoconstriction and hypertension, which can all decrease circulation and increase the risk of death even in calm water.'

'Correct.' He went back to his lecture.

I turned to Sidnee. 'Oops,' I said.

She sent me an amused smirk. 'I knew you had it.'

I focused on the lecture and this time I kept my wilful mind on the game. I didn't like being called out – I felt a total twat like Thorsen.

I did keep checking the clock though, as the lecture dragged on. Although the cold-water survival stuff was interesting, I'd rather have been out doing some snooping or snogging. I reflected on my own cold-water experience when we'd been chased by the terrifying kushtaka. Good times. After nine interminable weeks at the academy, I was *so* ready for a real case.

The lecture moved onto facts and figures about rates of survival. I wondered what a vampire's life expectancy would be in the deep cold, or if it would affect a full vamp like Connor. I knew I'd been cold when I'd jumped in the bay and had to be saved by our friendly water dragon, and I'd been almost unbearably cold when we'd jumped in the water to avoid the Otterman, but Connor had been an exceptionally strong swimmer. Didn't the cold affect him as much as me? I was a hybrid and there wasn't a lot of information about creatures like me, so I had to learn by doing. So far I'd learned that I didn't like cold water a whole lot, but I didn't know if it would kill me – and I wasn't keen on experimenting.

I checked the clock for the millionth time. Five minutes to lunch. I wiggled in my seat a bit; my bum was numb and I was getting super snoozy even with my soaking wet clothes. I needed blood and food. I'd have to run upstairs to get changed and drink some blood, but then I'd have time for a much-needed break.

I was so exhausted; the adrenaline of teaching had fired me up but now I'd crashed and my energy levels were in the toilet. So of-fucking-course, that was when Petty the Poltergeist came roaring back into the academy with a vengeance.

Chapter 23

The classroom door slammed open and an arctic wind rushed through the room, scattering books, paper and writing utensils. Students rolled around on their wheelie chairs then jumped up to seek shelter. Tables flipped and recruits were being pummelled by their own belongings.

'Everyone get out!' Fischer yelled. Trying to protect our heads, we rushed for the door. Several students had minor cuts and I was sure others had some nasty bruises. The lieutenant was the last out, and he looked the worst; he'd taken a beating. He shut the door behind him and shuddered.

Looking pale, Jones demanded, 'Sir, what the hell?'

'Someone left a hallway window open,' Fischer said firmly. 'It let in the bad weather. Now, those of you who need first aid follow me. The rest of you can go to lunch.' He stalked away.

Jones watched him go with a frown. 'This shit doesn't happen because of inclement weather,' he said slowly.

Danny shrugged. 'It's that or a ghost. Personally, I'm rolling with the weather thing.'

Jones shook his head. 'Something weird is going on.'

'Come on,' Danny said, changing the subject. 'Let's go eat.'

'We'll follow you in a minute,' I told him. 'I need to change out of my wet clothes.'

'Yep, that's two for two the weather got you!' Danny teased. 'See you in the food hall.'

Sidnee and I ran up to our room. Once we were alone, she looked at me wide-eyed and I noticed that her hands were trembling. She noticed me noticing and shoved them into her pockets. 'That's not good,' she said grimly. 'Petty hasn't even been gone seven days, and he seems more powerful than before. Bunny, I don't think we can force him out by ourselves.'

I shook my head. 'I don't either. We need to solve whatever he's upset about, then maybe he'll settle down or move on.'

'Yeah,' she said slowly. 'I think so too. But we have to tread carefully.'

'I hear you.' I squeezed her arm so she'd know I wasn't being flippant about her warnings; a poltergeist had taken family from her.

I filled a mug from a bag of O-, plugged my nose and guzzled it. Yuck; it was cold and gloopy. I was actually looking forward to warm blood.

Sidnee went into the shower to shift, and I stripped out of my soaking clothes to pull on some dry ones. I unfastened my hair, brushed and re-plaited it, then washed my face. Finally I looked presentable again.

By the time I was done, Sidnee was getting out of the shower, healed, clean and happier. 'Sometimes I love being a supernat,' she said. 'Well, okay – always!'

I agreed. It hadn't been my choice to become supernat. At the time I'd been happy as a human – although my job choices were definitely better now. I had hated being a waitress and constantly fighting off obnoxious, handsy customers. Maybe if I'd had my vamp fangs back then, they wouldn't have tried to take liberties. Whatever: I was much happier being a Nomo officer, kicking ass and taking names. Except for poltergeists who continued to kick *our* arses.

I hoped Petty had burned itself out, but we checked to make certain on our way to lunch. Sure enough, the classroom was as still as a millpond. We retrieved our things and put them on our desks. I thought about righting the whole room but we didn't have much time, so we straightened a few chairs as we walked out. It looked like a few other recruits had slipped in to do the same; most people here were good eggs.

Lunch was good – lasagna with salad and garlic bread – and the mess room was humming with chatter about the latest incident. Plenty of humans were scoffing at Fischer's explanation of bad weather, though they didn't have another explanation to offer.

I knew what was attacking us but I didn't know *why,* and without knowing that I couldn't stop Petty's temper tantrums. I needed to get back into the office and access his records. I'd have to break curfew and do it in the middle of the night; I didn't think that would be difficult, but I really didn't want to get kicked out of the academy for rule breaking if I got caught. How would I explain that to Gunnar? I was sure he'd back my choices, but if I got caught I could kiss goodbye to being a detective. The thought of that made my determination falter until I told myself to woman the fuck up.

When I'd finished eating, I sidled close to Sidnee. 'Hey,' I said quietly. 'I'm going back into the offices tonight. I've got to find whatever is setting off Petty.'

'I'm in,' she murmured back.

I blinked. I should have thought that through; of course she'd want to come with me, but I couldn't risk it. 'If we get caught, we'll both be expelled. You'd better stay in bed.'

'Fuck off, Bunny,' she replied conversationally. 'You're not doing this without me. So what if we get caught? Gunnar will understand. We won't lose our jobs, so how bad could it be?'

'Bad. I want to be a detective and I know you do, too. If we get kicked out, I doubt we'll be able to take any other classes. We'll be expelled with a big old red cross against our names.'

'So we'd better not get caught.'

I smiled ruefully; I loved the faith she had in us, but that didn't change the fact that we'd be screwed if someone came by or was working late. Luckily there were no security cameras, but there was a host of other things that could go wrong.

Sidnee was right, though: we stood a better chance if we worked together. One of us could act as a lookout – if we dressed in pyjamas, could we pretend to be sleepwalking?

It might look suspicious but they wouldn't boot us out of the program for sleepwalking, right? 'How well can you fake sleepwalking?' I whispered.

'What?' Sidnee frowned at me like I was mad. Maybe I was.

I waved it off. Okay, no to the pyjama plan. 'Never mind. We'll talk more about it in our room later.'

Fischer entered the lunch hall covered in bandages; he was escorted by Wilson, who was glaring at us like we had personally harmed his commander. My resolve to break into the office hardened. We couldn't let this continue because nobody was safe.

Chapter 24

I slipped to the bathroom then back to class. We were continuing our lessons on cold-water training but the food and blood had perked me up so I hoped my attention wouldn't wander quite as much.

Sergeant Marks was already there, replacing the head of the academy after the attack. I suppressed a pang of regret; I liked Marks but Fischer was much more experienced and his lectures had been my favourites. 'How's the lieutenant?' I asked quietly.

'A bit battered,' Marks said baldly.

'Can he shift?'

Marks shook his head. 'He's human.'

I didn't know why that surprised me; maybe I'd assumed that because Fischer knew about supernats, he was a supernat too. 'That was bad. Petty's getting worse,' I started.

'Yeah. We're going to have to do something. I guess I need to call in an expert.'

'Who you gonna call?' I asked lightly.

'I don't think the Ghostbusters are answering,' Marks said drily.

'Well, maybe we don't need them.' I bit my lip, wondering how much to tell Marks. 'Listen, I know something about the poltergeist. His name was Petrovich Peril and he was at the academy more than thirty years ago. He died of exposure after getting lost on a hiking trip. He communicated with me, told me that he thinks someone is undermining the academy somehow. He wants us to find out who and to stop them. He says his loyalty is to the academy. I honestly think if we can find out what he's talking about, the whole drama will stop.' Though to be honest, the death threat was weighing on my mind. What if I was wrong?

Sergeant Marks stopped tidying up and looked up at me. 'I see you've been doing some investigating on your own. Well, the academy is well-supervised and it would be difficult to do anything that would undermine it, so I can't imagine what Petty is talking about. The only thing we do in-house is the finan...' He trailed off and looked thoughtful.

'What?' I was burning with curiosity.

'Captain Engell,' Marks said slowly.

'What about him?' My heart gave a hard beat.

'He does the academy finances. They're the only thing that we really control on site.'

Was Marks suggesting that Engell might be embezzling? 'It did attack Engell's office,' I reminded him – the papers flying around had a tonne of numbers on them.

'Yeah,' he agreed grimly.

'Can we prove anything?'

He shook his head. 'I don't know. I wouldn't recognize a cooked book if someone hit me over the head with it.' He frowned. 'We need to bring in a financial expert to go over the figures – but if we're wrong, we'll offend a well-thought-of officer with ties to government officials and other high-up types. It'll be tricky.'

'Is Captain Engell really ex-MIB?' I blurted out.

Marks frowned, 'Where did you hear that?'

'Around,' I replied elusively. I didn't want Danny to get into trouble.

'Protecting your source like a good detective,' he said drily. He studied me. 'Yes,' he said finally, 'Engell used to be MIB.'

I bit my lip. That confirmed a whole other issue with Captain Engell. The financial angle was interesting, but the MIB had a whole lot of distrust toward supernaturals because they only dealt with supernats that had gone off-script. We weren't inherently bad but the MIB hunted those of us that were, so the organisation no doubt had a skewed perception of all of us. Was Engell here with an agenda?

I bit my lip. Thomas was ex-MIB, and he was a good person. Maybe the captain was innocent.

It looked like I was off the hook for late night B&E because I didn't have the background to know what I was looking at if this whole thing was financial. I'd seen a bunch of papers but nothing about them had seemed suspicious. Luckily it should be easy to find a forensic accountant who could interpret the numbers correctly.

Marks and I didn't get a chance to talk more because the other recruits were coming in. We quickly put the rest of the room straight and, although we were missing a few recruits who needed more medical assistance, Sergeant Marks started his lecture on time.

'We might not be going tonight,' I whispered to Sidnee once we sat down.

'Oh?'

'Yeah. Sergeant Marks gave me some insight.' I looked around to make sure no one was close enough to hear and whispered into her ear. 'They do the finances on site. Guess who does them?' I didn't wait for her answer. 'Captain Engell!'

'Damn.'

'You any good at forensic accounting?'

She snorted. 'My idea of forensic accounting is counting the dead bodies at a scene.'

I grinned. 'Same. Sergeant Marks is going to try to bring someone in on the downlow, so no breaking and entering for us tonight.'

'Roger that.' She gave me a thumbs-up as Sergeant Marks started talking.

Chapter 25

With our night-time escapade on hold whilst we waited for Sergeant Marks to find an accountant, all I had to do was plan my next demonstration with Fluffy. I called Connor after my supernat class to go over the next day's plan because I wanted his help. I was planning to do a demonstration of search and rescue and I needed someone to find. Connor was the obvious answer. He answered on the second ring. 'Hey,' I said. 'How was your day?'

I could feel his smile. 'It's only just started but it's all the better for hearing from you.'

'I can't wait to get onto a night schedule,' I admitted. 'I honestly miss it far more than I thought I would.'

'The daylight exhaustion complicates things,' he said sympathetically.

'Exactly! Without it I'd probably enjoy the sun but it makes me feel rundown, like I'm about to be hit with the worst cold of my life and I'm slogging through it.

Normally I cope fine because I get to mix up my days and nights, but nine weeks of days are killing me. Well, they would if I wasn't already undead. Kind of.'

'You can see why some vamps don't pay to buy the charmed necklaces. They're expensive and a symbol of status, but even though they help us go in the sun no vampire actually *wants* to go out in the sun. Don't get me wrong some vamps will still kill for one, so continue to keep yours hidden.' I fingered my necklace displaying my two pendants, Nana's triskele protection charm, and my daylight charm in the cheeky shape of a sun.

'Now that makes total sense!' I laughed. 'And that leads nicely to my next question. How do you feel about helping me tomorrow in the daylight?'

He laughed. 'For you, Bunny, I'll even brave the sun. What do you need?'

I had an atrociously soppy smile on my face. 'Fluffy and I are going to do a search and rescue.'

'So you need someone to rescue,' he interjected.

'I do indeed.'

'I'll be your damsel,' he promised.

'You're the best.'

'Don't you forget it. I'll meet you tomorrow in the parking lot.'

'Counting the hours.' I sighed. 'Love you.' I hung up before I could get even more sappy.

Eager to see Connor, I powered through my classes the next day even though nerves were nibbling the edges of my stomach. I was confident that Fluffy and I could do a good demonstration – after all, we'd done it in real life with the poor Savik brothers, and that had been truly scary shit. We'd done search and rescue *beyond* the barrier with a scary monster stalking us. This exercise would be a piece of cake in comparison.

I met Connor and shook off my nerves. Fluffy hopped out of the truck, his K-9 vest already in place and I greeted him with a full body cuddle and lots of pats. He licked my face enthusiastically, making me laugh.

'Lucky guy,' Connor muttered under his breath.

I turned. 'I can greet you just as enthusiastically if you like?'

He laughed. 'If you did, we'd miss the demonstration.'

My skin warmed. 'Right. Well then.' I cleared my throat and tried to sound businesslike. 'You have the undershirt?'

He reached into the truck and handed it to me sealed in a plastic zip bag. 'I wore it for twelve hours, as requested.'

'Thanks!' I covered Fluffy's ears, told Connor where I needed him to go, and he obligingly set off.

I released Fluffy's ears. 'I didn't want you to cheat and know where he was going,' I explained. 'We don't need to cheat to excel. Hard work will get us there every time.' Fluffy gave a firm bark, and we set off to show all of the recruits how it was done.

I felt more confident today when I was standing in front of my peers. Fluffy sat proudly next to me, eyes locked on mine, vibrating with tension. He was ready. So was I.

I turned to the recruits. 'Search and rescue dogs can be any breed – it depends on their strength and mental fitness to concentrate for periods of time. There are dogs that are specifically trained for avalanche recovery, seeking dead bodies and for finding a lost hiker, amongst many other things. Fluffy has a wide range of skills, and finding people is one of them.'

Danny raised his hand and I nodded to indicate he could ask his question. 'How do you know when he's found someone?'

'That's a good question. We'll demonstrate when we go outside, but part of having a trained dog is learning the dog's tells. I'm lucky because Fluffy is very demonstrative so he's easy to read.' Especially because he had human-level intelligence, but I didn't add that part.

When nobody raised another question, I continued. 'As we demonstrated yesterday, Fluffy has some skill with scent tracking, so I start with something saturated in the victim's scent. He also knows to watch and to listen for cries for help. That would help in an avalanche scenario, for example, or if someone fell down a mine, but he'd still track them first by scent since most of what he does is locating lost people.'

The recruits were taking notes, even Thorsen and his minions. Maybe Fluffy *had* impressed them a bit yesterday.

'I've set up a search and rescue situation. We'll go outside for the demo. Follow me.' I was pleased that this time that I managed to make it an order.

I'd asked Connor to hide in the woods behind the academy; he wasn't familiar with Sitka, but I figured a lumberjack would know his way around trees – and Fluffy would find him anyway. Besides, this was only an hour-long demonstration so Connor wasn't going to run at vamp speed and end up miles away. We needed to find him pronto and he knew it – not that he would make it too easy for us.

I had everyone gather at the obstacle course then pulled Connor's undershirt from the bag. 'Smell,' I told Fluffy. He sniffed it obediently and whined as he looked up at me. I winked at him – I doubted he truly needed the scent because he'd find Connor anywhere. 'Seek,' I ordered.

Fluffy put his nose to the ground and started in half-circles from our position. Since I'd made Connor walk through this area, he picked up the trail after three passes. I walked quickly to keep him on a loose lead. I drew the class's attention to his behaviour when he paused and looked back at me, then we followed as he trotted, nose down, through the trees behind the building.

The murmurs behind me sounded positive and I grinned to myself as I followed my dog. About a half mile out, Fluffy stopped, lifted a front foot and looked back at me. I waited until everyone was in earshot. 'You can see that he is pointing. He thinks our target is near.'

'Where's the missing person, then?' Thorsen yelled out obnoxiously.

'He's here, but first I'm going to free the dog to pinpoint precisely where.' I removed Fluffy's lead. 'Hunt.'

Fluffy put his nose down, walked ten steps and scratched at the ground. I frowned. What had Connor done? I'd figured he'd go up a tree or hide in the brush, but he was obviously being a little tricksier than that. *Vamp,* I suddenly thought; he'd be more comfortable hiding in true dark.

'Fluffy is indicating that the victim is underground,' I reported, starting to worry that something was off.

I tried to trust my four-legged friend and push down my jangling nerves as I walked to where Fluffy was scratching at the ground. It sounded hollow. I looked down and saw some loose earth covering some rough boards. It was obvious that the place had been disturbed very recently. Connor had found an old mine to play in.

Since I had to hide my freakish strength, I waved Danny over and together we pulled the boards free. Then, since we were all playing human, we both helped pull Connor out of the ground. 'You scared me,' I murmured quietly.

For a moment the fear that something had happened to him had vibrated through me. I remembered all too well finding him bound and gagged; the memory of that was still riding me, making me almost breathless.

He read the emotion in my eyes. 'Hey, it's okay. I was perfectly safe. The mine is sealed and there was enough space between the sealed part and the boards for me to lie down and wait for you. I knew you'd find me. Anyway, I could have gotten out on my own, so no harm, no foul.'

'You scared me,' I repeated softly, not quite sure why fear was still clawing at me like an alien trying to break through Sigourney Weaver. *Connor was fine. Everything is okay.* Even as I thought that, fear was still sliding down my spine and it took conscious effort to subdue it. What was going on?

I got back to work; I had a job to do and I was damned if I'd let Thorsen or his mates see me with my lip quivering. I pulled back my shoulders and turned to the crowd. 'Any questions?'

Several hands went up and I answered easily. From their questions, it was clear they were impressed and all of them wanted a K-9 companion. Who could resist a furry best friend?

We were done. Most people started back with Sergeant Marks, but Sidnee, Danny, Connor, Fluffy and I stayed behind to cover up the mine so no one would accidentally fall in. Before we could start, Danny hopped in. 'Hey!' I shouted. 'What gives?'

I moved closer to the hole to help him back out, but the irrational fear washed over me again and I stepped away from the edge. Danny was an adult and he was fine. I had no idea where this second-hand claustrophobia/mine-ophobia was coming from. I took some calming breaths and the fear slowly receded.

'I'm looking!' Danny said casually. 'I love mines!'

Men were so weird. Sidnee rolled her eyes at me in agreement.

Danny turned on his phone torch to have a good rummage around. I was still keeping my distance but I was watching him impatiently, so I saw when he stilled unnaturally before swiping something from the ground and pocketing it. 'What did you find?' I asked nosily.

'Just a fossil,' he replied casually.

I didn't believe him. 'You collect those, too?' I pressed.

'Doesn't everyone?' He flashed me a smile, but his eyes were tight and the tension in his jaw told me he was upset. I left it alone – for now. He probably wouldn't be open about any strong emotions in front of Connor since he barely knew him.

Danny climbed out of the hole and gave Fluffy some good-boy pats while Connor and Sidnee laid down the last of the boards. Danny was eyeing me curiously, noting the rigidity of my body and the distance I was keeping from the creepy hole.

Connor pulled me into his arms to give me a hug, one I found I sorely needed. I didn't even mind if it was caused in part by his own need to be a tad territorial in front of Danny. I trusted Danny and every single thing I'd seen from him had told me he was good people, but Connor didn't have that same experience.

'We'll go,' Danny said, amused. 'Give you some space.'

'Allllll the space!' Sidnee agreed. They walked away, leaving me alone with Connor and Fluffy.

Connor kissed me, sweeping me off my feet – metaphorically, of course, unlike Petrovich. As if I'd summoned him with my thoughts, a chill wind ran down my neck and I jumped away from Connor and whirled around. An amorphous blob was standing barely a foot away from me. 'Petrovich!' I exclaimed and scrambled back a little. The ghost's sense of personal space was way off.

Connor swore as he turned to face the poltergeist.

'Save our souls!' an eerie wailing voice howled from the wind then the apparition faded as quickly as it had appeared.

I shivered and wrapped my arms around myself. Fluffy had crouched down, too; only Connor was standing alert, ready to fight off something he couldn't touch. I appreciated his protection, but as far as I knew there was nothing he could do against a spirit.

'At least it didn't try to kick our asses,' he said drily.

'Yeah, I appreciate it a lot more when he *USES HIS WORDS*.' I said that last bit loudly, hoping the poltergeist would hear and obey.

'That was creepy. I can see why you're worried.'

I shuddered. 'He said "Save our souls". Does he mean SOS, that he needs help? Or does he mean we actually need to save his soul?'

Connor frowned. 'I couldn't actually hear his words, but you were closer. Still, I've never heard of a ghost being that coherent before.'

'Do you have a lot of experience with ghosts?' I asked curiously.

'No, but I've been reading a lot since I became your personal researcher.' He paused, 'Has anyone said anything to you about Liam Smith?'

I blinked. 'Who?'

'Recruit Smith. He was a part of the last cohort.' His expression was grave. 'Apparently, he left the academy halfway through the course.'

I shrugged. 'There are a lot of drop outs.'

'Sure – but this one never found his way home.'

Chapter 26

Connor told me what he knew about the missing recruit. Liam Smith had been a supernat from Ugiuvak, the other supernat town. I blinked at that: Danny worked for the Nomo's office there so he *must* have heard about Liam going missing.

Occasionally Danny had seemed so incredibly competent and knowledgeable that I'd thought that he really didn't need the academy except for some rubber stamping. Was he here to dig into Liam's disappearance? His weird reaction in the mine suddenly had a whole new meaning and questioning Danny moved high up my to-do list.

My mind was whirling when I said goodbye to Connor and hustled off to join Marks' next class: he'd forgive me being late because he knew I'd had to deal with my dog. I slid in at the back of the room and forced myself to focus.

The class was interesting but I was still relieved when it ended because questions were burning a hole in my brain.

The room emptied quickly as everyone rushed to lunch. I signalled for Sidnee to stay behind so I could tell her and Marks about Petty. When I recounted the episode with Petty, Marks looked grim. 'I've found a forensic accountant, someone discreet. They'll fly in tonight,' he said softly. He looked around to double-check that everyone else had gone. 'Captain Engell is teaching after lunch, so I'll try to sneak into his office then and look around.'

'Shouldn't we wait for the accountant?' I asked.

'I probably won't recognize anything, but it might be my only chance to dig into Petrovich's file. At the very least I can take some photos of the financial files for the accountant in case we can't sneak him into the office. That will be difficult because Captain Engell has been staying up late to catch up on the books.'

'When does he leave his office?' Sidnee asked.

Sergeant Marks shrugged. 'He says around ten. I'm usually gone by then, so I don't know precisely.'

I knew that because we wrapped up our supernat classes with Sergeant Marks at nine. Regardless of his plans, I was rapidly forming my own. Marks hadn't mentioned

Liam Smith going missing – maybe he didn't know. Either way, it was time for a vampire and her mermaid sidekick to snoop around after lights out. Okay, at first blush the mermaid thing didn't seem ideal, but Sidnee could turn her eyes black so she could see in the dark depths of the sea; her night vision was excellent, which made her the perfect lookout.

Marks continued. 'I guess we'll worry about it if I can't find anything.' He sighed.

I had one last question. 'Did you know someone called Liam Smith?' I asked casually.

'Sure, he was one of the supernat recruits last year.' He looked disappointed. 'I thought the lad had potential but he dropped out. Not everyone can handle the pressure. Still, it's better that they find out here than after they're sworn in.'

I smiled. 'You're right, I'm sure. Well, let us know how you get on with the accountant,' I said firmly. 'We're leaving it in your hands.' Like heck we were.

As we left. Sidnee slid me a sidelong glance. 'We're not leaving it in his hands?'

I grinned. 'Nope.'

'Who's Liam Smith?'

I filled her in on what Connor had told me as we hustled up to our room so I could grab some gazpacho blood to guzzle before lunch. 'You don't trust Marks?' Sidnee asked as I glugged down my coppery meal.

I wiped my mouth. 'It's not that I don't trust *him*, it's more that I don't trust anyone right now. All we know is that someone is trying to destroy the academy. Petty died here, and Liam disappeared. Sergeant Marks brought up the financial angle. He might be right – it could be embezzlement and maybe Engell *is* cooking the books. We need to check if he was a temporary TAC officer when Liam Smith was here. I don't know what's going on yet, but I think the answers are in that office, the one the poltergeist hit first. I'm going in tonight. Are you game?'

She nodded firmly. 'Absolutely. I'm your ride or die. Something is fishy, and not in a tasty way. I'm with you on this – I'm not sure who to trust, apart from you. I'm doubly not sure about an outside accountant because that could be another way to throw us off the scent. The accountant might tell us everything is hunky-dory when it isn't.'

'I hear you. Tonight, then?'

'Tonight,' she agreed. Her tummy let out a long rumble, making me giggle.

'Hungry, Sid?'

'Shut up!' She nudged me. 'Not all of us get tasty snacks in a fancy fridge! Teacher's pet!'

I snickered. 'It's not so much that I'm a teacher's pet, rather that Fischer doesn't want me to go into a bloodlust state and kill everyone. Small things like that.'

'Yeah, that would be frowned on. Best keep the vamp fed.' With that decided, we headed to lunch.

It felt like a long time until lights-out, especially as we were stressing about getting caught, but we needed our shot at that office. Even if we didn't understand the financial documents, we needed to determine who was trying to harm the academy. Aoife had said someone didn't have the academy's interests at heart, but what exactly did that mean? I hoped we'd find a clue; any clue would do.

I felt completely blind, like I was stumbling into who knew what, and I hated feeling ignorant. It wasn't something I'd experienced often because my prodigious memory allowed me to recall everything. With the added complication of Liam Smith's disappearance, the stakes had suddenly risen. Two recruits had vanished, and though Petrovich had been found he was dead. My stomach clenched. It didn't bode well for Smith.

I spent the day trying to get Danny on his own to question him about Liam Smith but someone was always around and I didn't want to raise their suspicions. I'd told Sidnee I didn't trust anyone, though that wasn't strictly true: I trusted her and I thought I trusted Danny. He'd always had my back where Thorsen was concerned and he'd called out Polk when he'd bullied Jones, not to mention lending me his handkerchief when my nose was bleeding like Niagara Falls. Annoyingly, I still hadn't managed to get it laundered and return it to him. I was carrying around the thing like a bloody memento, but at that moment laundry was low on my list of priorities.

Engell's afternoon class was as boring as his others had been he was dull as dishwater though he seemed competent and friendly enough. As class ended, he called out, 'Barrington, see me after class.'

The class made a juvenile 'ooooh' sound like I was in trouble and I rolled my eyes, making them laugh. 'You wanted to see me?' I asked pointedly when we were alone.

As he studied me, he suddenly looked younger, sharper and more dangerous. He flashed me a shark's grin. 'You know Patkotak?'

Surprised, I answered, 'Yeah. You?'

'Yes.' He leaned forward. 'Is there anything you want to tell me?'

I blinked, nonplussed. 'Like what?'

'Like about the damned poltergeist wreaking havoc on the academy?'

'Oh, about that? Nope.' I kept my tone light.

Clearly frustrated, he sighed and sat back. 'Speak to Patkotak. You can trust me.'

Really? I could trust him like the gingerbread man could trust the fox.

He sighed again. 'Dismissed,' he barked when it was clear I wouldn't engage further.

I stalked out, eager to get to my supernat class. On the way, I spotted Thorsen's broad frame crowding someone. I moved closer to see who he was bullying this time: Eben. 'Hey,' I said loudly. 'What do we have here? A budding bromance?'

Thorsen shot me a hate-filled glare and stalked off without a word; I considered myself lucky. I turned to Eben. 'You okay?'

He glared and pushed past me without a word of thanks. Charming.

'You're welcome!' I hollered at his back, but he ignored me. I grimaced; maybe he was upset at having a woman rescue him from a bully, or maybe he was upset that I'd joked about a bromance between him and Thorsen. Maybe next time I rescued someone I shouldn't insult them at the same time, but it had been Thorsen's fault; something in him brought out the worst in me. Everyone else seemed to think the sun shone out of his ass, but all I could see was the darkness in him.

When I filtered into our 'remedial' class, Eben was already sitting down and Margi was perched at the front. I looked at Marks and mouthed 'later'. He gave me a slight nod.

As always, I was excited about my supernat class. This one was about dwarves and I could have listened for hours.

'You'll know all about dwarves,' Harry teased Danny. 'You're a proper gnome, aren't you?'

Danny's expression went flat. 'Good thing we're friends,' he muttered, 'or I'd kick your ass.'

'I'm missing something,' I said. Danny was a huge beast of a man, which frequently amused me since he became extremely small when he shifted into a raven. But I didn't think there wasn't anything gnome-like about him – although I had no idea what magical gnomes were like. I'd only met the garden variety that Mum thought were terribly gauche.

'You're always missing something,' Eben jibed, his tone still distinctly unfriendly. Okay, so maybe I'd accidentally threatened his masculinity by rescuing him as if he were a damsel in distress. Should I apologise? I'd been trying to help.

Marks' voice cracked out like a whip. 'Enough! We're getting off course. Barrington, a gnome is a derogatory term for a person from Nome.'

Danny looked exasperated. 'It's a lame joke about our height.'

'I thought you were from Ugiuvak?' I was confused: Danny had *definitely* said he was from Ugiuvak.

'I live there now,' he assured me. 'But I was born and raised in Nome.'

'Okay... But you're really tall and gnomes are short, right?' I pointed out. He'd said it was a height joke.

'Most of us are,' Danny said. 'It's like calling a giant "Tiny". It's hilarious, it never grows old.' His voice was laden with sarcasm.

I grinned, enjoying learning some in-jokes. Marks rapped his knuckles on the board. 'We are here to talk about dwarves, not gnomes. Eyes front and centre, mouths closed.'

'Walk me to my dorm later?' I whispered to Danny as the class was wrapping up. Looking intrigued, he nodded. Apparently he hadn't been oblivious to my glances during the day. 'I need to speak to Marks,' I went on. 'Wait for me outside with Sidnee. I won't be a minute.'

I waited until the classroom was empty before approaching Marks. 'Anything?' I asked without preamble.

'Something,' he said grumpily. 'All the files for Petrovich's year are missing. The files for the years before and after are still there.'

'And the financials?'

'I took a tonne of photographs for the accountant so I hope he can spot something. There was an empty drawer, though, and it looked like it had been cleared out recently.'

'Engell is a neat freak,' I pointed out.

'Undoubtedly. I'll get the files to the accountant and let you know if anything leaps out at him.'

'Great.' I paused. 'Why are you letting me help you?'

He gave a wry smile. 'Firstly, it's clear you're going to look into it with or without me. Secondly, if we identify Engell as the culprit, you can take our evidence to Fischer for me and that way my job isn't on the line if we're wrong.' He looked serious. 'I like my job at the academy because I get to help promising young supernats make a positive impact on the world. That's more important than Engell stealing a few thousand dollars. What I do *matters*.'

I nodded. 'It does. Thanks for being frank with me. You find the evidence and I'll be your fall guy.' I paused. 'Engell pulled me in at the end of the class. He said we had a mutual acquaintance.'

'And?'

'Sidnee knows the acquaintance too, but he didn't call her in.'

'You think he was trying to pump you for information?'

'Maybe. I haven't been terribly subtle about my investigation. Anyone can check my library history and see what I've been looking into.'

Marks grimaced. 'Keep your eyes open and keep walking around in pairs.'

'You got it.' I gave a mock salute and went to join Danny and Sidnee. Danny nodded in greeting then jerked his head towards Sidnee. 'You trust her?'

'Fully,' I confirmed.

By silent agreement, we ducked into the other dark classroom. As Sidnee took up a position at the edge of the door to watch for interlopers, Danny switched his focus back to me. 'You've been trying to get my attention today. What's up?'

'Liam Smith.'

Danny tensed. 'What about him?'

'He was from your village.'

'He was.'

'You knew him?' I pressed.

His expression was grim. 'He was a friend.'

I studied him. 'Apparently he dropped out from here but never made it home?'

Danny's jaw tightened. 'He didn't drop out, I swear it. The records said he had, but we spoke the night before he went missing and he was real enthusiastic, overflowing with praise for Sergeant Marks.'

'Marks in particular?' I asked.

'Yeah. I got the vibe that Marks had taken him under his wing. Marks is a bear shifter, same as Liam, and Liam really looked up to him.' Danny's voice choked up.

I patted him on the shoulder. 'So that's why you're here? You're already a detective, aren't you?'

'Damn right,' he confirmed. 'My Nomo made out like there was a disciplinary issue and he wanted me sent back to school to re-learn all the basics.'

'But really you're undercover?'

'You bet. And something fucking stinks. Liam never mentioned an active poltergeist. And...' he paused '...I found this in the old mine.' He pulled out a ring. 'It was Liam's. Whatever happened to him, he was down there.'

'A squad challenge?'

'Maybe,' he conceded. 'But I can't help but feel that he was Hansel and Gretel-ing.'

'Leaving clues for you,' I mused.

'Something happened to Liam and that something happened here at the academy. And I'm going to find out what.'

I licked my lips. When I'd found Connor in the mine, I'd felt a fear that was off the charts. Connor had said hybrids could feed off auras, so what if I could sense emotions, too? The fear had been so overwhelming; what if it hadn't been my fear but the fear that someone held there had experienced? Someone like Liam Smith.

I kept my suspicions to myself because I couldn't even begin to express them without revealing my hybrid status, and if that came out it would be a death warrant. Instead I told Danny everything I'd learnt about Engell and Marks and what I knew about Petrovich.

Then I told him that Aoife had said someone was working against the academy's interests and reminded him of Petrovich's threat – or warning – that we were all going to die. Finally, I told him about Petty's comment about saving our souls and that I didn't know whether it was a warning or an entreaty.

All I knew was that something dark was going on. And we were going to get to the bottom of it.

Chapter 27

The three of us were now officially working together and it felt good to have another experienced person on the team. We sneaked down to the TAC office, but even though it was 10.30pm we could see the light was on from the big reception desk window. It looked like Captain Engell was still in there.

We retreated back to the breakroom between our dormitories. 'When should we try again?' Sidnee asked quietly.

'Let's give it until midnight,' I suggested.

'I agree,' Danny said. 'That way most everyone will be asleep, including the captain.'

'We'll go back to our room for now,' I said. 'That minimises the chance of us being discovered out of bed. We'll meet here again in another hour and a half.'

We separated from Danny to go into our dorms. Sidnee gave me a silent nod as she lay down on her bed and I guessed we'd brush our teeth and fangs later. I climbed into bed and turned so that we were facing each other. 'Listen, Engell told me he knows Thomas. Can you text him and get him to corroborate?'

She frowned. 'I can try but he's usually incommunicado when he's hunting someone down. I don't know when we'll get a reply.'

I shrugged. 'It's worth a try.'

She retrieved her phone and sent a message to Patkotak, then settled back down and looked nervously at me. 'What are we going to look for?' she whispered.

I wasn't sure, and that was the problem; it was Sergeant Marks who had suggested something financial might be going on. 'I don't know,' I admitted. 'I guess we're looking for anything out of place.'

'That's what I was afraid of,' she sighed.

'I wish Fluffy and Connor could come,' I said. 'We could use some more eyes.'

Sidnee half-sat up in her bed as an idea struck her. 'No way could Connor and Fluffy make it all the way in here because the security is too tight – but we do have other eyes! Why don't you see if you can call Aoife again? She might be able to sneak around the office unseen!'

Now that was a genius idea. 'That's inspired. Maybe Aoife can rope in Petty, too, so he can guide us to whatever the fuck we should be looking at?'

Sidnee grimaced. 'There is a fly in our ointment. Neither Petty nor Aoife are exactly quiet.'

'I can tell Aoife we need quiet. She can manage an incognito mode.' Probably.

'But can Petty?'

'Maybe not, but no one should be around to hear him. He's the one with all the freaking answers. If we can get him to lead us to something...'

She nodded. 'I hear you.' She paused. 'I really hope he doesn't lead us to Smith's body.'

'Me too – for Danny's sake.'

'Where do you want to summon them?'

Margi started to snore loudly and we exchanged amused glances. 'She sounds like a freight train. Please tell me I don't sound like that!' Sidnee joked.

'Your snores are more delicate, more like the rumble of a car on the road,' I reassured her.

'Hey! I was kidding! I don't snore!'

I laughed. 'You totally do, Sid.'

'Well, no one has ever complained about it!' she huffed, folding her arms.

'You're too pretty to be kicked out of bed for a little light snoring.'

'I am.' She flashed me a grin before sobering. 'We need to focus. Where are we going to summon Aoife?'

'In the offices – at least no one will be around if she arrives wailing.' I winced at the thought.

Sidnee rolled on to her back and stared up at the ceiling. 'Should we let Gunnar know what's up before we get our asses tossed out?'

'Nah, let's leave that as a surprise.'

'Everyone loves surprises, right? And they don't always have to be good ones!'

We chatted quietly until the clock rolled over to midnight and it was ninja o'clock, then we rolled out of bed and sneaked silently across the hall to wait for Danny. When he joined us, we slid downstairs in our stockinged feet. Sidnee and I were built for the night, so we led the way; we didn't need anything other than the illuminated exit signs to light our way.

It was quiet, almost too quiet. The recruits were asleep upstairs and surely Captain Engell was finally in his fancy apartment suite; at least his office light was out. Like before, I climbed over the reception desk to the office.

Sidnee was close behind me and Danny was bringing up the rear.

We took the key from the receptionist's desk and let ourselves into Captain Engell's office. Even with the door closed it wasn't totally dark because the light over the front door was streaming through the reception window and giving plenty of light for a mer and a vampire. Ravens were diurnal, but when I turned to Danny his eyes were glowing slightly. It looked like the shifter had his own skills.

I quickly explained about summoning Aoife and Petty. 'All right with me,' he said. 'As long as neither of them scream and get us caught.'

And wasn't that the kicker? I looked at Sidnee. 'You ready for me to call Aoife?'

She looked around nervously. 'Yeah. Do it.'

I whispered, 'Aoife I need your help.' We waited. Nothing happened. Bugger.

'Aoife Sullivan! Please come, it's important!' I said a little more loudly, although I wasn't sure that it was my voice that called her because I always felt a tug in my chest when I summoned her. Maybe it was my witchy power; some day I'd know all my own secrets, dammit.

This time a wind whipped around my braid and Aoife's pale form materialised in front of me. She had her translucent arms crossed over her chest and she was tapping her foot. Luckily, she was silent.

'Cool,' Danny murmured, and she flashed him a flirty smile.

I cleared my throat. 'Thanks for coming, Aoife. I know it's probably a pain, but we really need your help. Can you summon Petrovich for us? We have very little time to find out who is threatening the academy and how they're doing it, and we don't have a clue where to start. If you can get Petrovich to point out something, maybe we can stop whatever is upsetting him.'

By the time I'd finished, Aoife was looking intrigued. She opened her mouth. 'Don't say anything!' I said sharply and held up my hand. 'We have to keep quiet – but can you help us?'

She looked thoughtful then gave an uncertain shrug and faded from sight. Danny whispered, 'Does that mean yes?'

'I don't know. I *think* so. I guess we snoop around while we wait to see if the spirits are joining the party.'

We separated and started searching through the papers on top of the desk and in the drawers. There was an old desktop computer on the desk – next to a shiny silver laptop.

Sidnee, who was more tech savvy than me, opened the laptop and stared. 'It has a fingerprint scanner.' Then she smiled. 'But it also has this!' She held up a small sticky note. 'The password. This computer does either/or!' She lifted her hands showily, cracked her knuckles and typed in the password. 'I'm in!' she crowed triumphantly.

I squatted next to her to see what she was looking at: a file labelled 'Academy'. 'I'm going with door number one,' she said and clicked on it.

'What the *hell* are you doing?' An angry voice demanded. Uh-oh.

I looked up and mentally amended my 'uh-oh' to 'oh fuck!'.

Chapter 28

Sidnee and I lost any street cred we might have had when we both jumped a mile high. We'd been concentrating so hard that our sharpened supernat hearing had totally failed us. How utterly embarrassing.

Thorsen and his number one bitch, Miller, were staring at us from the doorway, their expressions thunderous.

Sidnee, Danny and I looked at each other as we wondered what to say. No matter what we did, these two bastards would try everything in their power to get us expelled or charged – or both, for that matter. Our options were to answer them and hope for a sympathetic ear, to tie them up and stash them in a closet somewhere – or to kill them. Number one was impossible, and we knew we weren't going to kill them, so the second option was the most appealing. It was up there with flying pigs and the Chudley Cannons actually winning.

Thorsen leaned against the doorway, his arms folded and a smug look on his face. 'I said what are you doing?'

Sometimes offence is the best defence, so I narrowed my eyes at him. 'What are *you* doing here? Do you have Captain Engell's permission?' The 'like we do' was implicit – and total bullshit.

Thorsen opened his mouth to snarl something that was no doubt witty and cutting, but before he could utter a word an icy wind whipped around the office and sent sheets of paper flying and pens swirling around us.

Saved by Petty Peril! Aoife had come through. The poltergeist wasn't interested in our company; he was laser-focused on his own agenda, which apparently was saving the academy. And this time, he was showing his actual form – or what remained of it. It was blurry and dark, but unmistakably human.

'Noooo,' he wailed as he tore through the room. Anything loose swirled around in a violent storm. 'Follow,' he howled – and I realised he was addressing me.

'You got it,' I said, a shade nervously. 'Lead the way.'

Danny, Sidnee, and I leapt up and ran after the debris as it raced out of the door. We shoved past Thorsen and Miller and scampered down the hallway. Thorsen's eyes were wide as he watched us chase the phantom. The two men followed at what I'd have called a cowardly distance.

The hallway only had two other doors: one on the left and a fire exit at the end. The door to the left led to the building's plant room and we'd been told during our orientation meeting that it was strictly out of bounds because it housed electrical equipment, pipes and dangerous compounds; it even had a sign saying *Strictly no entry*. Naturally, the debris arrowed towards the forbidden door. The ghost went through it, whilst the flying missiles stopped and dropped to the ground.

I tried the door; predictably it was locked.

Despite the warnings, it wasn't heavy-duty but a regular interior door; it was solid but the locks weren't special. Luckily, I didn't need any fancy lock-picking skills I had learned one lockpicking spell, after Connor's singular attempt to teach me lockpicking had failed.

Carefully blocking Thorsen and Miller's line of sight, I wiggled the knob while saying the words. That ball of heat in my core warmed some, and the handle turned. I opened the door. It swung open to show a stairway heading downwards. Great: creepy, dark stairway. Check.

There weren't usually basements in buildings on the islands in the southeast of Alaska because there too much water and sand; most were built on pylons that ran down to the bedrock. I could tell from the sounds coming up the stairs that these steps did indeed lead to the academy's forbidden plant room.

A long wail that sounded like 'follow' screeched up to us. We obeyed Petty's ghostly command and ran down into the darkness; after all, that always turned out fine for the heroes in horror movies.

'What do you think is down here?' Sidnee asked from behind me as we descended the stairs.

'The furnace and electrical box?' I said optimistically. I'd be so pissed off if it was a dead body; dead bodies were more of a 2am thing.

She slapped me on the back. Thanks to her supernat strength and my super-slidey socks, I slid down the next three steps. 'Oh shit! Sorry, Bunny! I meant what is Petty going to show us?'

'I don't know.' There was no need to panic her until I smelled death, and so far all I could smell was stale, musty air. Maybe Petty *did* want to show us an electrical box. Imagine if all of this was because Petty wanted the academy to use a greener source of energy; we could stop his haunting simply by installing solar panels—not that they'd work in the land of perpetual rain.

At the bottom of the stairs the corridor turned sharply to the left and a dimly lit hallway led into a large room that housed the heating and lighting controls. We looked around, trying to find evidence of Petty Peril but he'd lost all his debris at the door and we couldn't pinpoint his presence. At some point in his ramblings, he'd lost the human-ish form that I suspected had cost him a lot of energy to retain.

'We can't see you!' I explained to him. 'Do something to show us where you are?'

Nothing happened. Fuck. Had he dissipated before showing us whatever it was he'd dragged us down here for? Sidnee, Danny and I turned and started to search the room that was full of pipes, tanks and valves.

Thorsen and Miller came into the room and stared at us. Thorsen was red faced; we were ignoring him and he *hated* to be ignored. 'If you don't tell me what's going on right now,' he started, 'I'm fucking arresting you all.'

Sidnee rolled her eyes. 'Yeah, good luck with that. We're following the poltergeist, you idiot. Didn't you see him?'

'I didn't see anything but you assholes,' Thorsen said firmly, though his eyes were a little wild.

Sidnee moved closer to him; if she'd been taller, they would have been chest to chest. She prodded him and rocked him on his feet. 'You are a coward and a liar.' She punctuated every word with another prod.

Wow! Go, Sidnee! I guessed she was done pretending to be a soft little Miss Suzy. The problem was Thorsen wouldn't put up with that, not from her. He was a man who wanted his women to cower. If he tried to hurt her, I'd stop him – or she would – and things would get really messy. Maybe option number three wasn't out of the question after all.

Thorsen's face turned a mottled purple and his hands curled into oversized fists. The poor guy obviously thought he had the advantage, and it would have been laughable if the entire room hadn't been so tense. He gazed down at Sidnee, his lip pulled back in an almost animalistic snarl. 'You are a pushy little criminal.' His spittle flew onto her face.

'Jeez, Thorsen! Say it, don't spray it,' she shot back. She rolled her eyes and turned around to leave.

Several things happened at once. Miller moved around to block Sidnee from leaving, Thorsen pulled out a pair of handcuffs and grabbed Sidnee's arm as she turned, and Aoife materialised between Danny and me.

Aoife took in the scene, opened her mouth and let out a piercing banshee wail that made me slam my hands over my ears. I cried out as the noise cut through me. Miller was close to Aoife and, as a human, he took the brunt of the scream. He turned ghastly white and fainted dead away. Neither Danny nor I moved to catch him.

Thorsen was focusing on Sidnee and attempting to clamp the handcuffs onto her wrists. Sidnee, who'd truly had enough of faking human female powerlessness, turned on her heel and punched him in the face with her supernat strength. Thorsen went down like a sack of wet shit. She shook her hand and a small grin pulled at her lips. 'Man, that was intensely satisfying.'

I checked Thorsen's pulse; that had been quite some hit and he *was* only human. It thrummed under my thumb; yep, the prick was still alive.

'He's going to feel that when he wakes up,' Danny remarked. 'Nice one, Fletcher.'

'Sidnee, please.' She smiled.

Danny smiled back, 'Danny.'

'*This* is the time you two choose to get on a first-name basis?' I huffed.

Sidnee chuckled then sobered and toed the unconscious man. 'He's a problem.'

I sighed. 'Yep. He's going to make trouble about what he saw here tonight.'

Danny pulled out some zip ties from his pocket and tied Thorsen's and Miller's arms behind their backs. When I quirked an eyebrow at his extra equipment, he said, 'I used to be a boy scout.' My expression remained blank so he expanded, 'I'm always prepared.'

'Ah. Good to know.'

Danny gestured to the small trail of blood coming from Thorsen's nose. 'I know you're a new vampire, Bunny, but you seem to have a remarkable lack of bloodlust.'

'I drink blood regularly.' And also I was a secret hybrid who didn't have any bloodlust at all.

'Even so.' He eyed me again. 'My point is that you're still not thinking like a vampire. You can use some mind-control hypnosis. Tell them they slept all night then we'll send them back to their beds and no one will be any the wiser.'

I blinked. Could I mesmerise them? If *I* couldn't, Connor was still on Sitka for one more day. Maybe I could call him in to do the dirty work for me? 'I've never done it. Do you think I should call in my boyfriend? He's an older vamp,' I explained.

'What's his name?' Danny asked curiously.

'Connor MacKenzie.'

His jaw dropped. 'Jesus, you landed on your feet. He's not *an* older vamp, he's one of the oldest vampires in Alaska, not to mention heir to the throne of the US vampires.'

'Yeah. He's really down to earth, though,' I said lamely.

Danny looked amused. 'I'm sure.' His tone indicated he was anything but. 'Even so, we don't have the time or resources to smuggle him onto the campus right now. It'll have to be you.'

Me. Right.

Evidently Aoife'd had enough of waiting for us to work through our issues. 'Petrovich called me to help. He's over there.' She pointed, then led us to the far corner of the room. She'd learned to modulate her voice because her speech wasn't a screech; it sounded more human, though it still sent some spine-tingling terror racing down my spine.

We looked around the corner but still missed whatever we were supposed to see. Petty stirred the air and an icy wind encased us. Finally Aoife pointed to a spot under some large pipes. There, well-hidden, was a black attaché case. I ducked down and crawled on my hands and knees to pull it out.

Sidnee knelt down next to me, as did Aoife; she seemed to be as curious as we were. I went to flick open the clasps but Sidnee stopped me. 'Wait. It might be a bomb or something. What if you open it and we all go kaboom?'

I drew back and Danny snorted with laughter. 'This isn't a spy film. It's a case – it probably has papers in it.'

I looked at Aoife. 'Can you ask Petty if this is a bomb?' It never hurt to err on the safe side.

Aoife rolled her eyes. It was easy for the already-dead girl to be flippant but I wanted to stay alive – I didn't have a mysterious second life like she did. This undead one was all I'd get. She turned her face toward the wall and spoke, although we didn't hear anything, then she paused as though she were having a conversation, only we couldn't see the person she was talking to. After a few seconds she turned back. 'It's not a bomb.' The 'well, duh' was kind of implied.

I nodded, stared at the black case for another moment then flipped open the clasps.

'Well, what's in it?' Sidnee asked me impatiently.

'Papers.' Just like Danny had said. I drew out a bunch of files; stamped on the first one in big block letters was *TOP SECRET*. A cursory glance through the rest showed the same labels. I look at the words beneath; the group granted top-secret clearance was the MIB: the Magical Investigations Bureau.

I showed the first folder to Sidnee and she reeled back like she'd been slapped. For her, the MIB was the bogeyman she'd been told to be scared of for her whole life.

'What the hell is going on?' she whispered.

I licked my dry lips as I opened the first file and read the first few sheets. 'This is much bigger than embezzlement,' I breathed. 'Look.' I showed her and Danny the line that almost made my slow heart beat in time with Sidnee's. It read: *A plan to extract and experiment on supernatural entities through the use of the Alaska State Troopers.*

Fuck me sideways with a cucumber. This was *not* good.

Chapter 29

Whilst our eyes were fixed on the papers, Thorsen was struggling to sit up. His hands being cuffed behind him made it hard for him to gain purchase – but not impossible. His eyes fixed on the papers that we were poring over. 'Put those down! Our papers are not meant for your eyes!'

Our papers? Things were going from bad to worse. I dropped the files back into the case. 'You're MIB?' I asked incredulously. Suddenly it made sense: he could be an ass and a bully because he wasn't attending the academy as a recruit, he was a freaking spy! That's why he was never told off properly for his bullshit: he was from one of the alphabet agencies.

His terrible temper seemed real enough, though, so clearly that part wasn't pretence. His face mottled purple again, except for the nice swollen part that was already starting to show a sizeable bruise where Sidnee had decked him.

He sneered. 'Don't you dare talk to me! Don't you dare even look at me! I am worth a hundred of you! You're little more than *beasts,* and like any animal population spiralling out of control you need to be monitored – and then culled.' He smirked. 'I'm all too happy to do the culling.' He met my gaze. 'And I'm more than happy to start with you.'

My fangs dropped. They still had a mind of their own but for once they were appearing at the right time. I bared them in a fake grin. 'You want to say that again?'

His gaze flicked down to my protruding canines and I saw his Adam's apple bob as he swallowed. Even so, he kept up the bravado. 'You drink *blood* to survive. You disgust me – you, and the others like you. You should all be wiped off the face of this earth.'

He had a set of brass ones, that was for sure, and he was as stupid as two planks of wood, but he was certainly bold.

I looked at Danny's angry face, then back to Thorsen. 'This extraction plan. Is that what happened to Liam Smith?'

Thorsen looked blank. 'Who?'

'The recruit that went missing last cohort,' Danny snarled from between clenched teeth.

Thorsen smirked. 'Aw, was he your little best friend?' He shrugged. 'I didn't know him, but if he was a filthy supernatural then yeah, he'll have been taken for some experimentation. Like you guys will be. You've sealed your fate now.'

'Is Liam alive?' Danny pushed.

The twat shrugged. 'How should I know? Each course has different MIB operatives enrolled on it. We can't have people cottoning on to what's happening. The MIB targets someone supernatural, usually a species that's been requested.'

'And who's your target this time?' I asked.

Thorsen grinned. 'Why, it's you, my little rodent. You and your charmed necklace that tells anyone in the know that you're a filthy vampire. I knew what you were from the moment I set eyes on you – I didn't even need to be told you were supernat.' He stared at us. 'Now, untie me and I promise I won't arrest your families and loved ones and take them to a detention centre. Leave me tied up for one more fucking minute and I'll personally see them all in chains.'

He said it with absolute authority and my stomach knotted. For most supernats that would be a crippling threat, but I didn't have family in the US and I wasn't scared of him. I pulled out my phone out, thankful that I had a signal even down here, and called Connor.

'What are you doing?' Thorsen asked, his voice growing shrill as he realised I wasn't kowtowing to his demands.

Connor answered promptly. 'I need your help,' I said before he could speak. 'Can you talk me through how to mind control someone?'

Thorsen's eyes went wide. 'No! Don't you dare!' Danny cut him off by putting his large hand firmly over his obnoxious mouth.

'We call it mesmerising,' Connor said. 'It's not usually something we teach on the fly, but I'm assuming there's an emergency since you're calling me at one in the morning.'

'You bet.'

'Okay. Is your target human or supernat?'

'Human.'

'That's good.' He sounded relieved. 'Humans are a lot easier to mes because they have virtually no defences to speak of. The process starts with you. You need to search inward. Close your eyes and turn your attention inside your head.'

I closed my eyes and did as he directed.

'You should feel a power inside of you like a cold ball of ice.'

I had only ever felt heat within me but, sure enough, when I looked inside more carefully I felt an area of dense cold.

'You need to reach out to it and pull the power out from it,' Connor went on. 'Look into the recipient's eyes and release the magic, then tell them what you want them to do or remember.'

'Okay. Thanks.'

'If that doesn't work,' Connor said, 'you can try hitting them repeatedly on the head. A concussion will do the same thing in a pinch, at least until I can get to you.'

I found myself grinning. 'Aw, thank you.'

'And Bunny?'

'Yeah?'

'You're going to feel drained afterwards. Have you got someone there to help you get to bed?'

'Sidnee and Danny are with me.'

'Danny?' he asked lightly.

'He works for the Nomo in Ugiuvak. He's undercover, investigating Smith's disappearance. The problem is that the MIB are undercover too – but they're here to expedite disappearances.'

'Fuck,' Connor said. 'That's not good. Find out if the MIB prick has sent a report with your name on it. We need to know if you're a target.'

I swallowed. 'He's already said he was targeting me.'

Connor swore colourfully and extensively. 'All right. We need to do some damage control. Gunnar has a guy in the MIB. Leave it with me. Let me know if you can't mesmerise the MIB guy and I'll sneak in to join you.'

'Security is too high,' I warned. 'It's impossible.'

He snorted. 'I'm a vampire, Bunny. No security is good enough to stop me if I'm determined – and I'm *very* determined. There's nothing I wouldn't do to protect you.' With that modest comment, he hung up.

I pocketed the phone, closed my eyes and reached inwards for the cold ball of ice inside my brain. I pulled it upwards and out, then opened my eyes and met Thorsen's panicked ones. He didn't know enough to look away; thank goodness for small favours.

I stared into his eyes. If he hadn't been such a bastard, I'd have thought they were nice eyes. They were blue, not Connor's ice blue but a faded blue grey. They complemented Thorsen's whole 'master race' look – the pale skin and blond hair.

I held his eyes with mine and I somehow *felt* that he couldn't look away. Once I was sure of the connection, I spoke. 'You did not see the three of us tonight. You will not remember anything from after dinner until you wake in the morning. You will go to your bed and go to sleep. When you wake, you will be sympathetic to supernats. Now leave.'

Danny cut through the ties and heaved Thorsen to his feet. He swayed but then, without further ado, he turned and headed to the stairs. 'Wow,' Sidnee said, impressed. 'It actually worked!'

'Beginner's luck,' I noted drily. I didn't point out that her surprised tone revealed that she'd had precisely zero confidence in my abilities. Frankly, that was fair.

She stared down at the still-unconscious Miller then shoved him with her foot. 'Let's see if Thorsen was a fluke.' He groaned and she gave him another gentle kick. 'Get up, you ass.'

He rolled over. This time, the kick was a little more serious. 'Ow!' He came to, sat up and looked around wildly. 'What did you do to Theodore?'

'Absolutely nothing. He went to bed. As will you.' I met Miller's eyes and searched again for the cold spark of power. 'You will go to bed and you will forget everything from dinnertime until you wake up in the morning. You will be sympathetic to supernats from this moment on. Now go.'

Danny cut through Miller's ties and pulled him up. Freddie turned and headed for the stairs. 'I guess I won't make you mad anytime soon,' Danny told me with a grin.

Suddenly I felt drained – it was like being hit by the daylight exhaustion but times a million. Even breathing felt like hard work. 'I don't want to do it again right now,' I said drily. 'So you're safe.'

Aoife was still floating a foot off the ground where she'd been speaking to Petty. She was watching us. I turned to her. 'Thank you, both of you.'

Danny nodded. 'Petrovich Peril, you have done a service to all the supernats that will pass through this academy and probably to all those who live in the great state of Alaska. Thank you.' He gave a sharp salute. I needed to learn how to do that.

The air around us warmed and for a second a young man appeared in the corner dressed in his state-trooper uniform. He smiled and snapped back a salute, then his image blinked and a brown bear appeared in his place before fading from view.

'Has he left forever?' Sidnee asked Aoife.

Aoife shook her head slowly. *Not yet,* she mouthed. Whatever: he was obviously calmer now that we'd understood what he'd been trying to tell us.

'Petty was a shifter,' Sidnee said wonderingly.

Evidently so, which made me wonder how a bear shifter like him had supposedly died of exposure in the woods. Had it been foul play? A dark thought came to me: how long had the MIB been operating out of here? How many recruits had been kidnapped or killed? The supernats' natural suspicion of each other and their total lack of information sharing made them vulnerable.

Aoife faded soon after Petty and we stood alone in the plant room. 'I'm exhausted,' I managed.

Sidnee yawned. 'Yeah, me too. What are we going to do with that?' She pointed at the attaché case.

Danny frowned. 'We need to read the contents and copy them, if we can. We can take turns snapping some pictures of the pages. Once it's in the Cloud, it doesn't matter if anything happens to this lot.'

Or us, I thought darkly.

'That's a *lot* of pages,' Sidnee sighed.

'We'll have to go through them tomorrow, see if there is any dirt on anyone else at the academy,' I suggested. 'We need to know who the enemy at our gate is besides Thorsen and Miller.'

Danny lugged the case back to our room and I buried it in my closet. Sidnee and I said our goodnights then collapsed on our beds.

Tomorrow was going to suck.

Chapter 30

Sure enough, when my alarm went off I knew even blood wouldn't revive me enough to face the day. Exhaustion dragged at my limbs and every fibre of my being wanted to roll over and go back to sleep.

I couldn't though: I still had a lesson to do with Fluffy, still had the attaché case to look through, still had Sergeant Marks thinking this was all a school finance issue – and I still didn't know who we could trust. As a former MIB, Engell was right up there as a suspect, but the thing with Patkotak was giving me pause, unless Engell knew that Patkotak was on a hunt and couldn't be contacted.

The conspiracy theories were making my head spin. Knowing that the MIB was behind everything made me trust Sergeant Marks a little more, although I knew that the MIB did employ *some* supernats so he wasn't completely in the clear.

We mustered, did PT with a grumpy Wilson, then had a takedown test with Blake before class. I was anxious to see how well my attempt at vampire mind control had worked, so I kept Thorsen and Miller firmly in my tired gaze. It felt odd when Thorsen strolled in and didn't barge into my shoulder; he still looked at me, but his gaze wasn't filled with the usual vitriol.

But whatever fates existed, they certainly had it in for us. First to do the mat test were Sidnee and Thorsen – and Thorsen had a very distinct bruise on his face. If my mesmerising hadn't worked...

'I don't know how it happened,' Thorsen was saying to one of his friends. 'I must have fallen out of bed.' He was frowning as if he didn't quite believe his own explanation, and with good reason: it was total bullshit.

In the end, the takedown between Sidnee and Thorsen was fairly routine. Both of them toed the line and, for whatever reason, Sidnee let him win. He didn't crow in triumph or shove her around, so I guessed I was officially competent at mesmerising. Go me.

I shivered a little; it wasn't a skill I really wanted.

Danny and I were paired up and passed our test with flying colours. Naturally.

When we were dismissed for breakfast, I ran up to the dorm, took the case from my closet, flipped through the top folder and started taking pictures of each page. I hadn't gone far when Danny and Sidnee joined me.

'Hand me another one,' Sidnee said.

'And one for me,' Danny added. I passed them both a file.

'Scan-read for now and look for familiar names,' I instructed. 'We're trying to see who we can trust.' After a few moments, I huffed in annoyance. 'There's nothing in mine.'

Sidnee finished a few minutes later. 'Me neither.'

'Nor this one.' Danny sounded discouraged. 'It's talking about subject blah-blah and reeling off a list of numbers, but nobody identified by name.'

I glanced at the clock. 'That'll have to do for now. Let's go to breakfast before anyone gets suspicious.'

After I'd slugged back my cold blood, we ran down to the cafeteria. 'I'll look at another file while you're getting ready for your Fluffy lesson,' Sidnee said.

'Thanks.'

'Then maybe I can slip away while you do your thing with him. I don't think anyone will notice,' she suggested.

I considered it before nodding. 'Okay, it's worth the risk. It won't be long before someone realises the papers have been taken.'

'I've sent the pictures we've already taken to my Nomo so he can start examining them,' Danny said.

'Great.' I didn't suggest sending them to *our* Nomo. Gunnar had enough on his plate, and the last thing he needed was me dropping some sort of conspiracy into his lap.

When I went to get Fluffy, Sidnee slipped upstairs for another round of file photographing.

'Everything go okay with the mes?' Connor asked as I strolled out to meet him.

'Mes?' I asked, momentarily confused.

'Sorry. Mesmerising.'

'Oh.' I blinked. Duh. 'Yeah, everything seemed okay. I told them to forget the whole thing and to be nice to supernats.'

Connor frowned. 'Were they nice to supernats before?'

'No. They were assholes.'

Connor's frown deepened. 'I'm sorry, I should have said. Making someone forget is easy enough but making them change a long-held attitude is all but impossible.'

I thought of Thorsen's lack of a shoulder barge. 'It does seem to have taken, though.'

'For now,' Connor warned. 'It'll start to unravel soon. Hopefully their lack of antagonism won't be noted and flagged up to the wrong person.'

Shitsticks. I hadn't thought of that. I led Fluffy out of the car and gave Connor a brush of the lips goodbye. 'Keep your eyes peeled, Officer Barrington,' he ordered me as I walked away.

'Like prawns,' I agreed, making him smile.

Once again, I took the recruits outside for my demonstration. When we'd assembled, I started talking about finding drugs but my heart wasn't in it. I kept thinking about how fisheye had devastated Portlock and led to Connor losing his number two, Juan Torres. I'd liked Juan.

The idea of the MIB kidnapping and experimenting on supernaturals had me doubting what we'd always assumed, that the black-ops team hadn't been sanctioned. Maybe the whole thing was an MIB-sanctioned project that sought to contain or cull supernats as if we were *animals*. The thought was making me feel sick and my focus on the demonstration just wasn't there.

Halfway through the demonstration, Sidnee slipped into the back of the group. She mouthed something to me but I didn't catch it, then she hopped nervously from foot to foot, which distracted me. At the end of the demo she followed me to the truck to return Fluffy to Connor. Once we were alone, she couldn't contain herself any longer. 'It's Lieutenant Fischer,' she blurted out.

Fuck: that was as bad as it could get. The head of the academy was involved? He was human, but he knew about us supernats.

As soon as we joined Connor, I told him about the documents. 'We're still going through the attaché case but can you take it back to Gunnar when you leave Sitka?'

Connor's eyes flashed. 'If you think I'm leaving you here alone when you're in danger, you have another thought coming.'

'Please, Connor. You need to take it to Gunnar or the Nomo in Ugiuvak. There might be something they can use to track down the black-ops group that was peddling fisheye in Portlock. And it will definitely help get the word out to the other communities.' I hesitated, not sure if what I was about to say would go down well. 'And maybe you need to let your dad know, too.' Fisheye was deadly to vampires.

Connor's eyes snapped back to mine. 'My father? No.' He shook his head firmly.

'He can tell all the vampires in Alaska to be careful. I was the target this time, Connor.'

'Even so, we don't want my father to be thinking about us or Portlock – or even the whole of Alaska.' There was no time left to discuss the matter. 'I'll handle it,' he said, but the anger was rolling off him at the situation we'd found ourselves in and the big old target on my back.

I didn't want to leave it like that but I had no choice; I was due back at class and I didn't want to raise suspicion any further. 'Come by tonight and we'll bring the attaché case out to you.'

Connor nodded, though he wasn't happy. I reached up and kissed him gently, then turned to my four-legged friend and thanked Fluffy for his hard work. He'd really carried the afternoon since I'd been exhausted and darn right spacey.

'Be careful, Doe,' Connor entreated. 'Your lieutenant will be missing that case at some point.' He climbed into the truck and motored away, still looking pissed off. I didn't blame him; I felt pissed off, too. Someone had us in their sights – and it was because of *what* we were, not because of our actions.

Well, fuck them: we'd show them how wrong their ignorance was.

Chapter 31

Danny, Sidnee and I stole fifteen minutes from lunch to look through more of the files. I was sure we were missing a lot by skimming but our time was so limited. Frustrated, I threw my file back into the case. 'Any other names you recognize?'

'Not in this one,' Danny sighed. We both picked out another file.

Suddenly Sidnee yelped. 'Hey, you guys! This one names several high-ranking politicians in Alaska, including one whom I'm assuming is Thorsen's daddy.'

'Fuck,' I swore.

'We've got to get this info to our Nomos,' Danny said urgently. 'This is big – it may need a meeting of Portlock and Ugiuvak. The only way we can work through this is together.' He was right: this was way too big for us three to deal with alone.

I returned my folder to the case. 'I don't see Sergeant Marks' name anywhere – I think he's clean.'

'Clean enough to bring him in on this?' Sidnee asked.

I considered it for a minute but in the end I shook my head. 'I think it's safer if we keep it between us. This knowledge is dangerous and I don't want to put Marks at risk, even if he's clean.' The sergeant's comments about his job had stuck with me.

Danny nodded. 'I agree.'

I licked my lips. 'Connor pointed out that Fischer is going to be missing these documents soon, so we need to hide the case somewhere and get the documents out of the academy. We've only taken pictures of a quarter of the files so far – this is taking too long. The longer the files are here, the more danger there is that we'll be found with them.'

Danny frowned. 'What I don't get is why they were stashed in a utility room behind some pipes.'

I'd wondered about that, too. 'I think they were originally kept in Engell's office. One of the desk drawers was emptied recently and there was no dust. I figure that when Petty hit the room twice, Fischer decided to hide them somewhere out of the way. Where better than the plant room that we're not allowed to enter? You can't have top-secret documents floating around in a poltergeist storm.'

'That's definitely possible. So where do we hide the documents until we can get them out?' Danny asked.

I racked my brains. Everywhere except the TAC officers' rooms was open to the recruits. Our footlockers and closets were supposed to be private but anyone could get into them if they wanted to; I could open a footlocker without much effort, and even humans could do it with the right tools. *Think outside the box, Bunny,* I said to myself.

'The bathroom?' Sidnee suggested.

I shook my head. Our bathroom was pretty open and it would only take two minutes to search.

She went on, 'I was thinking where I'd avoid looking if I were a guy. I wouldn't want to go into a woman's bathroom. Throw a few pads and tampons around and they'll turn tail, right?'

Danny snorted. 'We're not that delicate! I've pawed through worse in searches.'

I glanced at the clock: we had three minutes before our presence was demanded. 'Okay, let's go with misdirection. I have a rucksack with a load of pockets and one of them is concealed. Let's put the contents of the files in there and shove some tampons and snacks in the other pockets. Hopefully nobody will dig around enough to find the hidden compartment. We'll leave the rucksack in plain sight – nobody will be suspicious of something that's out in the open. Then we fill the attaché case with loose papers and stuff it in a cupboard in the break room. If it's found, nobody will suspect us because everyone has access to the break room.'

Danny whistled. 'That's pretty darned ballsy.'

Sidnee grinned. 'It's so bold, it might even work!'

We leapt into action. Sidnee pulled the documents out of the files whilst I dug out my rucksack. It was hot pink with an animal print on it; I freaking loved that bag because it reminded me in a good way of the glittering lights of London and the life I'd left behind.

I stuffed papers inside it as fast as they were handed to me. Once we'd finished, the rucksack was only half full so I put a jacket over the papers and threw in all the packaged snacks we'd saved and a bunch of Sidnee's sanitary supplies. When it was full, I zipped the bag closed and went into the break room. Luckily it was empty; the other recruits had already cleared out and gone to class.

I leaned the duffel against one of the sofas, then opened a cabinet and shoved the attaché case full of fake papers to the back and replaced the food items in front of it.

'Hey, Bunny?' Danny asked quietly.

'Yeah?'

'Where did your nickname come from?'

Sidnee giggled.

'When I was little, before I was a vamp, I was actually a shifter. A were-rabbit.'

Danny snorted. 'I call bullshit. I've never seen someone so fascinated by our "remedial" lessons. No way you were born supernat.'

I grinned. 'How about this one? I have a wild, hoppity fighting style so my Nomo nicknamed me Bunny.'

Danny grinned. 'You're taking it to the grave, huh?'

'Something like that.'

We raced downstairs and walked into class two minutes late. Captain Engell frowned at us but he was in the middle of his introduction, so we didn't get told off. The lecture was an overview of forensic accounting, and it was also the final day the guest captain would be with us. If he was involved and he was gunning for me like Thorsen had said, then I might face a kidnapping attempt today. With that in mind, it was hard to focus on Engell's droning voice.

I'd thought the subject would be boring but I did find some of it interesting, particularly the descriptions of how the authorities found money that criminals had hidden. It wasn't an in-depth lecture because forensic accountants were specialists, but it gave us an idea of what they did and when we'd need one.

As the lecture was ending, Lieutenant Fischer came into class to announce a surprise squad challenge that would take place after dinner. I found myself looking at him in a whole new light and it was hard to keep the censure off my face. I couldn't imagine how anyone could hate someone else so much, whatever our differences.

I focused on his words and kept my gaze on my notebook. The squad challenge was a scavenger hunt in the woods behind the academy and I suddenly realised that it was probably an excuse to get the recruits out of the building so that he and Engell could search for the missing documents. Thank goodness we'd hidden them – but was hiding in plain sight going to work or bite us on the arse harder than the were-bunny I'd pretended to be?

Our hiding place *had* to work because I wouldn't be able to go back inside the academy until the squad challenge had finished. Connor had messaged and he was coming back at 10pm.

When Engell dismissed the class, he met my eyes and raised an eyebrow, tacitly asking if I'd heard from Patkotak. I shook my head and walked out; I wasn't giving him chance to get me alone because I trusted him about as far as I could throw him.

Fischer herded us into the mess for dinner; no one was allowed to slip away, not even for a moment. We had to act normally since he sat next to Margi and Eben; it was obvious to me that he was sitting with the supernats to keep all of us in his sights. He knew: he knew one of us had the case.

After we'd finished eating, Fischer led us out to start the challenge. We split into our squads and gathered behind the building for our instructions: we had to locate five landmarks marked on a map using only the map and a compass – no modern tech allowed. Once we found the places, we had to take a squad selfie and the first squad that returned to the starting point won.

The prize this time was an extra two hours in bed while the rest of the recruits scrubbed the building from top to bottom. It was a great prize because no one liked cleaning duty but everyone had to do it. If I hadn't had a kidnapping, a poltergeist and an evil government organisation looming over me, I might have even given a fuck.

'Okay, who's the best with navigation because I'm out?' I asked, once our group had gathered together. Navigating by map was a weakness of mine; before I'd come to Alaska, I'd been a big city girl and I only navigated via Google maps.

Jones raised his hand and the rest of us nodded. Although he was timid, he'd been the reason we'd won the last squad challenge. Besides, no one else had volunteered.

We'd been given old-school cameras for the photos, so there was no chance we could use our phones and 'accidentally' check the satnav. 'I'll take the pictures,' I volunteered.

We sent Jones to get the map and compass. Each squad had been given a different order in which to find the landmarks so we couldn't simply copy each other. We had ten minutes to prepare to search for our first landmark. When the whistle blew, four squads raced up the hill and into the woods then veered off in different directions. I hated letting Sidnee out of my sight.

It was autumn and the light faded early. We had head torches since it would probably be full dark before we returned, and one squad member had a large flashlight so we could take pics in the dark; even with the camera's flash, it would be hard to get a good photo without a proper light source.

I turned on my head torch when everyone else did, even though I could see just as well without it. Appearances were important.

Unsurprisingly, Jones did exceptionally well in leading us straight to the first spot. I took our squad photo then he mapped out the second location, which we reached just as Sidnee's team was leaving. We exchanged grins before she jogged off.

As we raced to landmark three, my anxiety started to fade. We'd hidden the papers well; our ruse would work and we'd get the evidence safely to Portlock. I kept that outcome firmly in my mind. I'd *manifest* it, dammit.

I checked my phone: just over an hour until Connor was back and I could slip him my duffle bag. It looked like we'd have finished the squad challenge before he arrived.

We took our photo and waited for Jones to lead us to landmark four. As we started after him, I heard someone mutter, 'Where's Danny?'

My heart froze as I looked around. I couldn't see him. 'Hey guys, hold up,' I called. 'We have to wait for Danny.'

I prayed with all my might that he'd stepped behind a tree for a piss, but the longer we waited the less likely that seemed. One minute passed, then three. Shit, this was bad, really bad. What if Thorsen had been heading me off the scent? What if *I* wasn't the intended target but Danny was? What if they'd already secured him somewhere? 'Danny!' I shouted, then we all started calling.

As we retraced our steps, we met up with Sidnee's group at landmark three. 'Have you seen Danny?' I panted desperately. Her eyes widened as she shook her head.

Danny was officially missing, lost in the woods on an exercise – like Petrovich.

Chapter 32

The supernat recruits started to find each other; we had superior abilities, so it made sense that we'd work together to search. Eben was a shaman and Margi a water witch, but Harry and George were shifters: Harry was a caribou and George was a wolverine. Since I wasn't familiar with those animals, I didn't know how well their noses worked but they had to be better than human ones.

I grabbed Margi. 'Margi, is there any magic you can do to help us find Danny?'

She grimaced. 'Oh shucks. I'm sorry, Bunny, but truthfully I'm not much of a scryer. If I had something of his I could at least do a lower-level seek spell, or I'd happily try to. Jeepers creepers, this is a mess.'

I thought about the scrying I'd seen in the past. It had really taken it out of a witch who had been an expert. 'Will it hurt you?'

'It'll wear me out, but I should recover after a night's sleep. It's not as intense as a true scry – but it's also not as effective.'

I dug out Danny's handkerchief and handed it to her. She looked at the object for a beat then shook her head and handed it back. 'Sorry, Bunny. It's covered in your blood. The only thing I could scry from that is you.' Dammit!

George came over. Keeping his voice low he said, 'I think I picked up a scent, but I'll do better in my other form.' He looked around. 'Cover for me, please, and hold on to my clothes. Don't let anyone shoot at me.' He looked nervous.

'We've got your back, Georgie,' Margi said firmly. 'Go ahead, petal.'

He slipped behind a tree and dropped his clothes, then a strange creature waddled out and my jaw dropped. I'd honestly thought wolverines were some sort of small wolf, but no; this wolverine looked like a badger or otter hybrid. He had dark fur and cream-coloured stripes that went from his jaws around his sides and ended in a short bushy tail. He wasn't large – and he wasn't like a wolf at all. I'd heard wolverines were fierce. I stared at dubiously at George; the wild ones might be fierce but he was adorable.

'Oh my,' Margi said, eyes wide. 'What a cutie!'

George looked up at us then went to the right. We followed. He chose a spot and snuffled around a bit before waddling off in a straight line; he had definitely scented something. Thank goodness he and Danny had roomed together long enough for George to recall his room-mate's unique smell.

Carrying George's clothing, I ran after the rest of the group. It was totally dark now and we were far away from the other recruits who had headed back along the route we'd come along. George was heading perpendicular to the trail we'd made on the way to the fourth landmark. He continued about a hundred yards before he stopped, snuffled and put out a clawed paw to scratch at something.

Sidnee knelt down and directed her head torch. 'It's a syringe,' she said, despair in her voice as she reached out to pick it up. Thinking of Gunnar and the fisheye, I yelled, 'Don't touch it, not without gloves!'

Everyone froze, even George who'd uncovered it with a bare paw. 'Are you feeling alright? Any strange sensations, sick stomach, hallucinations?' I asked him.

He backed up two steps and shook his head.

'Anyone have any gloves on them?' I demanded. No one did. I looked at George. 'Can I use your undershirt?' He had an undershirt and an overshirt, so I figured he could spare it. He gave a distinct nod.

I used the material to pick up the syringe and examined it. It had definitely been used recently and liquid was still dripping from the needle. I was careful not to touch it or let the blue-tinged, clear fluid that was soaking into the shirt touch my skin. I could smell blood when I lifted it near my face. We could only assume it had been used on Danny.

'George, do you mind shifting back so we can ask you questions about what you can smell?' I asked urgently.

He looked at his clothes then headed behind a tree. I set his clothes next to it and we turned our backs as we waited. He came out as he finished dressing.

'Thanks. So, why did you stop here?' I asked.

'The scent ended. If you look over there, you'll see four-wheeler tracks. That's all I could smell after Daniel's scent finished.'

Sure enough, there was a well-used track next to the spot where he'd found the syringe; a four-wheeler had veered over to this spot and the syringe had been pressed into the earth by its wheels, which was why George had had to dig it up. Whoever was responsible for Danny's disappearance must have dropped it accidentally and not noticed when they drove off. If I'd had any remaining doubts, they had gone. Danny had been kidnapped.

'What do we do?' Margi asked. 'Should we tell the sergeant?'

A chill went down my spine. I still wasn't sure if we could trust anyone in charge of the academy. Even though Sergeant Marks was a supernat, I had no way of knowing for certain if he was involved.

Sidnee and I exchanged a look. 'I think we need to follow this trail before they get too far away or we might never see Danny again,' I said, skirting the issue.

Sidnee backed me up. 'I agree. Which way did they go, George?'

He pointed down the trail: great, they were headed towards town. I wished one of us could fly, but that was Danny's skill and he'd been taken and drugged. 'Margi, you and Eben go back to the academy. If we aren't back in an hour, tell Sergeant Marks,' I said finally.

Margi nodded. Eben looked surly as usual, but they were basically human when it came to running through the woods and they knew they'd hold us back. 'Let's go, Eben,' Margi said, and they turned and headed back.

George, Harry and Sidnee looked at me. Connor would be here soon. It would be great to have him, Fluffy and a vehicle as well. 'Sidnee, do you have your phone?'

She patted her pocket. 'I've been keeping it on me in case I heard from Thomas about Engell.' What a little rule-breaker!

'Okay, I'm going to rendezvous with Connor and Fluffy. I'll text you from Connor's phone. Ping me your location when I do and we'll join you.'

The three of them hurried off down the trail. I watched them for a second then turned back to the academy and started to run.

I couldn't shake the feeling that Danny was running out of time.

Chapter 33

Connor wasn't there when I returned and my internal sense of time told me he was about five minutes away. I wasn't sure what to do. Should I go into the academy and retrieve my rucksack or wait until we'd found Danny? I refused to consider that Danny would have any other fate than being safely found. I was *not* prepared for Petrovich Part Two.

Recruits were coming back into the academy. By now all of the officers must have been informed about Danny's disappearance so the search for the attaché case had to be over. I wondered if the decoy would be missing from the break-room cupboard; if so, would my rucksack be missing, too? I hoped that all of the commotion would keep them from looking too closely at the attaché case's contents.

Just as I was about to make a decision, Connor's small white truck turned into the drive and started up the slight incline. I gestured for him to park and raced over to meet him. He got out and Fluffy and Shadow followed.

I scooped up the kitten, who was easily nine or ten kilos now, and he rubbed his furry face against mine. A raspy purr filled my ear. 'What's this?' I said, noticing his adorable Nomo vest. It was identical to Fluffy's, though it said 'Nomo Feline' instead of 'Nomo K-9'.

Connor winked. 'I thought he should have something since he's part of the team.'

I hugged Shadow again; I hadn't realised how much I'd needed to see him. 'You are so handsome in your vest.' I kissed his head before he started wriggling to get down, then he rubbed against my legs.

'So what's up?' Connor could read the tension in my body.

'Danny was kidnapped during an exercise.' I looked around to make sure no one was close enough to overhear, but we seemed to be alone. 'There was a surprise exercise so that Lieutenant Fischer and whoever is working for him could search the building for the documents we stole.'

'Did they get them?' His brow wrinkled with concern.

'I don't know and I can't check right now. Can I borrow your phone?' Connor passed it over and I texted Sidnee. 'Sidnee is going to text us her coordinates and we'll join them in the search for Danny. Whoever took him has drugged him and hauled him off in a four-wheeler. We need your truck.'

'You got it,' Connor assured me. 'I'm sorry about your friend. We'll find him.'

I gave him a hurried kiss. Thirty seconds later, the coordinates appeared and I ruffled Fluffy's ears. 'We're gonna need your help, boy. Are you up for it?' He gave a determined bark and his ears pricked forward; he was ready and eager.

I looked at the map on Connor's phone; Sidnee and the others were back on a paved road. 'Let's take the truck,' I said, showing Connor the location.

Fluffy jumped onto the seat and I held Shadow on my lap. Connor shut the door then climbed into the driver's seat; it was a tight squeeze with all of us in the cab.

As we pulled onto the main road, Connor put the pedal to the metal and soon we were back with my three friends. They looked dispirited, stumped about where to go next. Connor found a safe place to park off the road and he, Fluffy and I got out. I made sure Shadow stayed in the cab; the last thing I needed was to lose my intrepid cat as well.

George was staring into the distance and I wondered if he'd lost the scent. 'What happened?' I asked.

'We don't know which way they went after they left this trail,' Sidnee told me.

'George? Anything?' I pressed him.

'I think they went this way.' He pointed to the right. 'But the vehicle scents are overwhelming so I'm not sure.'

It was time for Fluffy to shine. I pulled out the handkerchief Danny had lent me after Thorsen had punched me. 'I know it smells of my blood,' I told Fluffy, 'but it should have Danny's scent on it, too. Can you decide which way we should go?'

He sniffed the handkerchief and the trail George had been following, then gave a happy bark and a wag as he snuffled this way and that across the grass. Finally he trotted forward, lifted his nose in the air and sniffed pointedly. He looked to the right and moved into his pointing stance.

I looked down the road; it went along the coast. 'Anyone know anywhere they could go down there?' No one did; none of us were local and we hadn't had a chance to explore the area. I sighed – I should have got Jones to help. Unless we saw the four-wheeler, there was no way of knowing where it was because there was a row of buildings along the road. It could be hidden in any one of them.

We piled into the truck. Sidnee, George, Harry and Fluffy got in the back and my dog stood in the corner against the cab with his nose in the wind. Shadow climbed into my lap to look out of the window.

After a couple of miles Fluffy barked once and pointed his nose at a warehouse on the water. Connor stopped and turned around; although there was almost no parking, he found a spot. As we climbed out of the cab I tried to shut the door on Shadow but he was having none of it and he followed us out. Connor attached a lead to his harness and handed it to me. I looked at him questioningly. Since when did Shadow have a lead?

Connor flashed me an exasperated look. 'Later. It's a whole story.'

O-kay, then. Fluffy barked and raced ahead, and we followed. Sure enough, behind the building was a camouflage-coloured four-wheeler. Connor put his hand on the side of the vehicle. 'It's still warm,' he murmured. 'This is it.'

I gave Fluffy a pat and a 'good boy'. He licked my hand then pointed towards the four-wheeler. Shadow went up to it, sniffed then hissed.

'What's the plan?' Sidnee asked as we all stared at the back of the warehouse. I looked at Connor.

'We go in, but we do it smart,' Connor said. 'Bunny and I will go first. Sidnee, wait three minutes before you and the others come in. Are any of you shifters beside Sidnee?' he asked. Harry and George nodded. 'Predators?'

Harry shook his head. 'Caribou.'

'All right. That's not very discreet, so stay on two. And you?' he asked George.

'Wolverine.'

'Great! Shift before you come in. Fluffy will stay with you.'

Fluffy whined and gave me puppy-dog eyes. 'Sorry, boy,' I told him. 'We need you to help Sidnee and the others.' His tail dropped and he looked at Shadow.

'I should put Shadow in the cab first,' I said to Connor, but the second I tried to pick him up my lynx went wild, flipping and jumping to try to escape me. I sighed. 'He won't go.'

'He has a mind of his own.' Connor's tone was dry. My curiosity was piqued again about this 'whole story' he hadn't yet told me, but now was not the time.

I handed Shadow's lead to Sidnee and he stood quietly next to Fluffy as Connor and I approached the door. Connor gestured for me to get behind him. In the weak light from the streetlamps, I could see that his fangs were down and I wished mine were smarter and would also drop. I had more control over them than I'd had before but they still didn't always appear when I wanted them too. *Now, you stupid teeth. Now,* I thought. Nothing.

Connor counted down on his fingers, one, two, three, then twisted the doorknob. It opened.

The warehouse was brightly lit and we blinked as our eyes adjusted to the brightness. Danny was sprawled on the ground. I started to rush forward but Connor caught my arm. 'Wait,' he hissed.

I looked up. Oops. We were surrounded by five men dressed in fatigues and holding rifles and sidearms. We'd startled them but they quickly levelled their guns at us.

'Who are you and what are you doing in here?' the tall red-headed man on the left demanded.

Connor and I looked at each other and then, as though we'd planned it, he went left and I went right, both of us travelling at full vamp speed. Connor had his knife out and slit two throats before I hit my first guy. I didn't have a weapon but I ripped away his rifle and hit him over the head. Connor knocked out a third soldier and I took down the last one with the butt of the gun.

I stared at the blood then up at Connor; he looked like an avenging god. His hair was dishevelled and his fangs were in full view as he snarled.

I didn't know who these men were or if they'd deserved to die, but it felt like they did. *Set aside your personal feelings, Bunny,* Gunnar's voice echoed from my memory. He was right – he was always right. These guys were doing their job, and right now their job was war on me and mine. They knew the risks.

Now wasn't the time for a treatise on morality. I wanted Connor, my friends, my pets and myself to live more than the kidnappers and I was ready to do anything to make that happen, to get us all out alive.

Just as the last guy fell, Sidnee and the others ran in. 'Check the rest of the warehouse,' I bellowed and we spread out. There were two more men in a back room with a speaker blasting rap tunes. Sidnee sneaked up on them, banged their heads together and they went down. In wolverine form, George streaked past us to an open door and I heard a shout from inside.

George had the man down. He slashed his legs then worked his way up the man's body until he was nothing but bloody pulp. Now I understood more about wolverines – cute, my ass!

'Bunny!' I heard Connor yell, panic in his voice.

My heart gave a firm thump and I ran out to the main room of the warehouse.

Chapter 34

'What's wrong?' I asked as I raced to his side. Connor was staring down at a case, though he wasn't getting too close to it. I swore loudly: it was full of small plastic bags full of hot-pink crystals. 'Fisheye.'

'A shit tonne of fisheye.' He backed away from the deadly drugs and ran his hands through his unruly curls.

I raced to Danny's side. If he'd been given fisheye, we needed to get him to healer or a hospital – now. In a pinch, maybe Eben could help – he was a shaman – but I wasn't sure if all shamans could heal like Anissa? By all accounts she was extraordinarily powerful; that was why I'd met her in the first place.

I calmed myself and *thought*. 'The liquid in the syringe was blue. Danny probably wasn't dosed with fisheye.'

'Blue?' Connor frowned. 'What colour was the other drug? The one that made you forget?'

'Amneiac? It was purple.'

He relaxed visibly. 'Good. That means they didn't wipe Danny's memory. He might have something helpful to say when he comes around. His heart is beating strongly so I don't think he's in immediate danger. Let's round up the living soldiers and subdue them, then we'll see if we can wake him up.'

Connor picked up two of the men and dropped them in the middle of the floor. Sidnee and George, who was back in his human form, brought out two more and Harry brought out the rest. The caribou shifter was hella strong.

I looked anxiously at Danny. He still wasn't coming around, although his chest was rising and falling with each breath. A couple of the soldiers we'd knocked out were stirring. Connor chose one of them and dragged him over to a chair. Luckily, the kidnappers had supplied us with rope and duct tape, so Connor tied his victim to the chair while the rest of us secured the others.

I went back to Danny to see if I could wake him. I was getting anxious seeing him lying there. I shook him gently – nothing. I dragged him over to a wall and propped him up against it. His head lolled but he still didn't stir. I checked his pulse; as Connor had said, it was strong and Danny was continuing to breathe without help. It looked like the blue drug was intended to knock him out rather than kill him.

I looked up. 'I don't know what else to do.'

Connor growled, 'We find out from this fucker.'

The man in the chair groaned as he came around. I stood in front of the chair and leaned down. His eyes took a minute to focus but then I saw recognition in them; since I didn't know him, that took me aback. 'You know who I am?' I asked.

He didn't answer. 'You know *what* I am, then,' I demanded. He blinked involuntarily; not only did he know what I was, he was frightened of me. Good.

My teeth clicked down as the bastards finally did what I wanted – I'd have cheered if the situation hadn't been so dire. I smiled, showed them to the soldier and he blanched. 'What did you give my friend?' I demanded.

He was breathing hard, panicking. 'I can't tell you. They'll kill me.'

Standing behind him, Connor laughed. The man tried to turn to look at him but Connor placed a hand on each side of his face to stop him moving, then he leaned down and growled in his ear, 'Listen to the nice vampire or I'll show you something to be afraid of.'

I guessed we were playing good vampire, bad vampire. 'What my darling mate is trying to say is that they *might* kill you but we definitely *will*.' Oh shucks: I wasn't a success at playing the good vampire. I gave my best movie-vampire hiss, teeth out and everything – and the sharp smell of urine filled my nose.

'It's called somnum,' he blurted out. 'It keeps shifters down for four hours. That's all I know!'

Somnum? That was Latin for sleep. These guys were as original as fuck. 'Is that all it does?' I pressed.

'Yes! At least, that's what they told us,' he amended.

'Who's your leader?' I turned sideways so he could see the pile of men tied up in the middle of the floor.

'The redhead.'

The only redhead was the man who'd had his throat slit, so we wouldn't be getting any more from him, not without Liv. I'd never thought I'd miss the terrifying necromancer but at that moment I definitely did. 'Is there a second in command?' I asked.

He shook his head; damn, this guy might be as good as it got. 'What were you supposed to do with Danny?'

'Who?'

'The shifter you drugged and kidnapped.' I was growing increasingly frustrated and my voice was tight. The man in the chair tried to lean away from me but Connor was still behind him.

'We were supposed to deliver him to this warehouse and wait.'

Connor was already moving. Sidnee, Fluffy and I joined him, leaving George and Harry to watch the inside of the warehouse. Sidnee thrust Shadow's lead into Harry's hand – he looked totally bemused to be suddenly responsible for a cat – and we burst out of the door.

We looked around to see if we were about to be overrun. Like our warehouses in Portlock, this one was next to the water with a dock behind to load and unload boats. It was still and quiet, and fog had rolled in to obscure the view. It was both a help and a hindrance: no one could see us, but we couldn't see what or who was creeping up on us.

'Fucking fog,' Connor swore as he scanned the area.

Sidnee leaned against me and whispered, 'I can swim out and see what I can see.'

I considered her offer. I didn't think she'd be seen but it would put her in danger. As a mer, she changed more than her form when she shifted: she became shark-like, violent, uncaring, the complete opposite of the sweet, shy, caring Sidnee that I knew. That switch also made her more impulsive and likely to get involved when she should remain hidden. I wavered; we needed the intel, but more importantly I needed her to be safe.

Before I could tell her not to, she started stripping her clothes. 'It's not a good idea,' I said.

'It's not safe, Sidnee,' Connor added.

Sidnee looked up with her black mer eyes and walked naked onto the dock before diving neatly in the water. I gathered up her clothes. It looked like she was done listening. Fair enough – we all had those days.

Fluffy gave an uneasy whine and looked down the row of warehouses to our right. I couldn't see anything in the fog, but I'd learned to trust his senses. 'Connor,' I whispered, 'Fluffy senses something down there.' I pointed.

He nodded and together we slipped around the side of the warehouse and waited. Fluffy was silent, his body tense against mine.

I knew when the men grew closer because I could hear low voices and the crunch of footfalls on the uneven ground. 'How many?' I asked quietly.

Connor held up seven fingers; he was a pro at differentiating heart beats.

'We've got to warn Sidnee.' I looked at the dock but I couldn't see anything. Even the single light at the edge of it only pierced the fog a few feet.

Connor pointed. An outline of a man appeared, then another, and their voices seemed to float towards us. 'Why isn't Anderson answering his walkie?' one of them asked.

'He's probably watching cat videos,' somebody replied.

'Nah, he's only into porn,' a third said. Disembodied laughter floated in the air.

The man in front suddenly stopped and held up his hand. 'Silence! Something is wrong.'

They went quiet. Now they were closer, we could see the whole group. They were armed and dressed like the others and they were on high alert. Just then, there was a slight splash as Sidnee emerged from the water.

She walked naked down the dock and seven guns swung her way.

Chapter 35

I started to run to my friend but Connor stopped me. He didn't look as stressed as I felt: he trusted Sidnee to be okay. I trusted Sidnee all day long – it was the men with the guns I was worried about.

'Who are you and what are you doing out here in the nude?' one of the men yelled. The fog was so thick that I couldn't tell which one spoke.

Sidnee hurriedly tried to cover herself with her hands as best she could. 'I'm naked because of a shitty prank.' She stifled a sob. 'Some bastards stole my clothes. Can anyone see them?' Her voice was small and wavering. She should have got an academy award.

'We're asking the questions.' The man's voice was sharp.

She flinched. 'We were all going skinny dipping but the others got out, took my clothes and ran off. My phone was in my jeans. Can you call for help for me? I'm freezing.' She shivered hard for effect, which was a sneaky trick because I knew she rarely felt the cold.

The guns wavered; at a gesture from the one who'd yelled out, they were pointed away from Sidnee towards the ground.

My friend looked around nervously like a naked young woman would do and pointed to the nearest boat. 'I'm going to check there for my clothes. They have to be stashed somewhere.'

The man nodded and she climbed aboard the fishing boat. Sidnee was shapely and gorgeous, so she had their *complete* attention. Idiots. Her clothes weren't on the boat because I was still holding them. I hoped she'd use the time to slip back into the water and get to safety.

Once she was on board, the men lost interest: she was some local yokel with bad judgement and they weren't there for locals. It wasn't even an issue that she'd seen them walking around with weapons: after all, being visibly armed in Alaska wasn't unusual when there were bears and wolves to think about.

The men relaxed and walked casually towards the warehouse; their rifles slung over their shoulders. Unfortunately for us, the jig was just up. Once they looked inside, they would declare war and we'd only brought our supernat selves and one knife to a gunfight. We needed to do something, fast.

Connor gestured for us to move behind the men. As long as we were silent the fog and the darkness would hide us, but even with vamp speed I doubted we could take any of them down before the rest turned on us.

Connor grabbed the first man. Putting his hand over the guy's mouth, he snapped his neck and laid him down carefully on the gravel. I took the next one and silently choked him until he passed out. We were down to five. I knew we wanted to interrogate the leader so we needed him to be the last man standing – and breathing – but he was in the middle of the others.

Fluffy thought faster than we did. He ran ahead silently then stood in the one spot where weak light almost hit the ground. He yipped then limped forward once the men had noticed him.

'Hey, it's a dog.'

'He's hurt.'

'He's wearing a collar. Shouldn't we try to phone his owner?' It seemed that even evil henchmen liked dogs.

'Ignore it. We have a mission,' the leader snapped.

'I like dogs more than I like you,' another man muttered mutinously.

'Shut up, Humphrey, before Grayson shoots you.'

Fluffy's distraction was helpful but not quite enough. As they moved past my dog, the leader looked around then stiffened and swore when he noticed that two of his men were missing. With a sharp command, the troops were back to being fully armed and alert as they stood back-to-back and searched the foggy darkness for us.

Nuts. There was no way we could get to them before they opened fire. I motioned to Connor that we should back away; I was out of ideas and, by the frustrated look on Connor's face, so was he. Fluffy was locked into his fake limp until we made a move, though no one was looking at him as he faded into the darkness. He was also making a strategic retreat: smart dog.

We were all on Team Sneak Away, except we'd forgotten the trickiest member of our team, Shadow. He must have slipped free from Harry because suddenly he was slinking past my leg. I tried to grab him but, like his name, he was mist, fog – and he was *hunting*.

I shivered as smoky colour lifted from his silvery fur and melted the cute harness right off him. He raced along the ground, enveloped two of the men and they went down screaming, as acid-like smoke consumed them. The other soldiers looked on in horror, as did I. Memories of the beast from beyond the barrier besieged me, and I fought for a moment to get back to the here and now.

When I looked at my lynx, unlike the beast he still retained his golden eyes. For the billionth time I wondered what my sweet boy really was. I didn't want him to be a killer; I wanted him to remain an innocent kitten, not become a murderous, deadly beast. This was *our* fight and it wasn't a supernatural one because the men were human.

Nevertheless, this was our chance and we rushed the remaining soldiers – but I tripped on an uneven patch of ground and the sound of me stomping on the gravel had them whirling around. Fucksticks!

Connor killed his target and Fluffy knocked another man down, but the leader had his gun aimed right at me. I tried to step aside at vamp speed as it boomed but I hadn't fully regained my balance. Connor stepped in front of me and the bullet went through his side.

As the blood seemed to spray in slow motion, my heart stopped and terror filled me. I wanted to throw up but I rushed to his side instead. He'd taken a bullet for me. My God, *he'd taken a bullet for me!*

Connor didn't even hesitate before reaching out to the man closest to him, the one Fluffy had knocked down. He opened his mouth wide, latched on to his neck and started to drink. Fluffy was wrestling with the leader, holding on to the man's wrist so he couldn't aim his gun at me again. As Connor drank to heal himself, I gathered myself and leapt into the fray.

I tore the gun away from the leader's grip but it was on a strap around his neck, so when I yanked it he went over backwards and pulled me down with him so that he, Fluffy and I were tangled in a pile of limbs and guns.

I threw a few hard punches, expecting him to defend himself and scramble backwards, but he let them land then moved towards me. He straddled me and pressed his rifle against my throat. Fluffy bit him on the ass and tried to pull him away, but although the guy yelled he didn't let up the pressure on my windpipe.

Shadow padded over and hissed but his smoky coat was back. He didn't have a lot of energy left after he'd deployed his shadow, so he probably couldn't use it to kill again.

I realised I was trying to take in panicked breaths like a human – but I wasn't a human. I was very *not* human. I met the man's eyes, reached into the cold part of my brain and shoved my will at him. 'Stop!' He froze. 'Lift your gun away from my throat.' Captured by my mesmerising magic, he did so.

Connor prowled forward, death in his eyes. 'Connor, stop! We need answers!' I yelled before he could rip the leader's head off. He stopped and ground his teeth.

The man was panting and blood was pouring from his mouth. My few punches had been solid and I reckoned I'd cracked a rib that had punctured one of his lungs. I had no time to be sympathetic, though, because we needed answers.

I held onto his eyes. 'What are you doing here with the supernats?'

'We are experimenting with some new drugs that will control you filthy supernats. We need more of you to experiment on because you keep dying on us. We were told to take more subjects from the academy because no one would report it.'

Connor barked, 'Who are you working for?'

'Answer him!' I ordered when the man didn't reply.

'I'm MIB. We're working for a secret black-ops group that doesn't have a name – at least, not one I know.'

Connor and I looked at each other grimly. 'And what's your objective here?' I asked.

'I told you. We're taking some of the supernat recruits from the academy for experimentation. We especially want the vamp.' His eyes remained on mine even as he hacked and coughed up more blood. Panic filled his eyes; he needed medical attention or he'd die – and he knew it.

'You can't have her,' Connor snarled. With a lightning-fast movement, he reached out and snapped the man's neck with an audible crunch.

Sidnee ran over. 'Are you okay? I couldn't get to you because they'd have seen me.'

'Don't worry. I'm glad you stayed safe.' I handed over her clothes. 'We're fine, but we've got a lot of bodies to deal with. What should we do?

Connor looked at Sidnee. 'You feel like another swim?' he asked.

She swallowed, and when she spoke her voice was unnaturally high. 'You want *me* to get rid of the bodies?'

'Is that possible? Won't they float up eventually?' I asked. We'd had the cold-water survival class but no class on what happened when someone dumped a body – or several.

Sidnee smiled and this time she showed her shark teeth; she was on the edge of going mer. 'Not if I put them in the Alaska current. They won't surface until they hit the Aleutians, and by then they won't surface at all.'

I shivered slightly at the change in my friend, though not enough for her to notice.

'You two drag them down to the water,' Sidnee said. 'I'll reappropriate a net and pull them out with me.'

'Reappropriate?' I asked.

She winked. 'That's law-enforcement speak for steal.'

I looked at the pile of bodies then back to my slender friend. 'That's a lot of weight,' I said dubiously.

'I'm a mermaid,' she replied flatly.

I knew what she was but I didn't know the true extent of her abilities because we'd never talked about stuff like that. Perhaps we should ... later. 'Okay.'

'What about the guns?' Her black eyes grabbed the tiniest bit of light from the weak street lamp and flashed.

Connor shrugged. 'We'll throw them in with the bodies.'

With George and Harry's help, we spent the next half hour dragging bodies and guns to the water. Not one soldier was left alive, and I found that hard. Clearly it had been them or us and I understood that choice intellectually, but emotionally I was struggling.

I decided to think about it later, much later when we were safe. Mer-Sidnee, Connor and George seemed perfectly fine with the body count, although Harry was looking a bit green. I was sure that Sidnee would also be green later when she was in her human form again.

We waited inside the warehouse while she did her thing. I sat cross-legged next to Danny with an exhausted Shadow collapsed in my lap, hoping Daniel would wake up soon; by now, he had to have been out for close to four hours.

He came round about thirty minutes later. He was disorientated and I had to explain a couple of times where we were and what was going on. 'Where are Margi and Eben?' he asked.

'We sent them back to the academy. Why?'

Looking grim, Danny shook his head. 'We need to get to Margi! She isn't safe.' He staggered to his feet. 'The person who stuck me with the damned needle was Eben.'

Fuck.

Chapter 36

'Eben?' I repeated. I was in a state of shock. He was one of *us*. Why would he harm us? Was he MIB too? The thought made me sick, but some supernats *did* work with the MIB.

That tickled something at the back of my mind and I thought back. The first time Eben and I had met he'd said he was a witch then he'd later claimed to be a shaman. He'd said he was from the village where Danny had grown up, Nome, but they'd never given the slightest indication that they'd ever met before. I'd put that down to it being a big town; I certainly didn't know every Portlock resident. But the truth was, Eben may never have set foot in that village. In fact, I couldn't think of a single occasion when he'd done anything supernat at all. Not ever.

George and Harry also looked shocked. 'Has Eben ever performed magic around any of you?' I asked slowly. They shook their heads.

Dammit, he was a plant. Had I inadvertently let anything slip about the attaché case in his presence? I skimmed my memories: no, I hadn't, thank goodness.

The only thing that stood out about Eben was his secretiveness and quiet judgement, even during supernat classes. We'd accepted him without question, despite his dour demeanour; well, more fool us. The MIB had needed someone within our group because supernats were hard to bring down; they'd needed someone to get up close and personal with us to take us down without killing us. I felt sick. The whole time Eben had been working against us.

How had I not suspected his involvement? Great detective I was turning out to be. The State Trooper Academy was being overrun by the MIB and they were removing supernats and handing them over to a shady black-ops group. They were planning to turn the Alaska State Troopers into a Gestapo group to eliminate supernats. I felt like I'd been dropped behind enemy lines in World War Two – or World War Three, for that matter.

'We have to get back,' Danny said urgently. 'Margi has no one to look out for her.' Not only was Margi in danger but the papers were at risk every second we delayed. But we couldn't go yet because Sidnee was still hip-deep in body disposal – literally.

'We can't leave Sidnee,' Connor said before I did.

'Yeah,' I added. 'She's taking care of *our* business and she's vulnerable if any more MIB show up.' The MIB had to have a ship somewhere out there and there could be a lot more of them aboard. We were sitting ducks.

Then it hit me: we'd killed MIB, and/or some of the black-ops group. My heart gave a single hard thump. 'We especially want the vamp,' ran through my head. We were already on their radar and they'd been planning to kidnap me.

My legs felt weak. If Connor hadn't reached out and rested his hand in the small of my back, I might have fallen. His presence, his love and his steadying hand shored me up, and my legs stopped shaking. This was no time for me to freak out; we needed to find Sidnee and get the hell back to Margi.

The door to the warehouse swung open and we all jumped. Connor leapt in front of me – but it was a wet and naked mermaid. 'Uh, what's up?' she asked curiously, as though we hadn't sent her out with a bunch of bodies and weaponry to dispose of. Her eyes were soft brown and her teeth normal. My Sidnee was back.

I hurried over and handed over her clothes then stood in front of her to give her a bit of privacy, although it was clear she couldn't care less. Once she was dressed, she wrung out her hair and quickly braided it.

'We need to go,' I said urgently. 'The short version, Eben is one of *them* and he's alone with Margi.'

She reeled back. 'Eben? Quiet Eben? But he's so sweet.'

That hadn't been my experience because he'd hardly connected with us, but this was Sidnee and she thought most people were sweet. 'It turns out he wasn't so sweet after all,' I said grimly.

We hurried back to Connor's truck. The three men and Fluffy climbed in the back, and Sidnee squeezed into the cab with me, Connor, and a sleeping Shadow. We took off, wheels spinning as we sped back to the academy.

'We need a story, something about what happened to Danny that the humans will understand.' I'd been worrying about that ever since Danny had woken up. We couldn't tell the truth so we needed something believable to keep Fischer off our radar. He needed to think we were still clueless.

I reached behind us and opened the sliding window that went through to the back of the truck. 'Hey,' I called. 'We have to get our stories straight for the humans.'

'I'll say I fell, hit my head and got lost wandering in the wrong direction,' Danny offered. 'Fluffy tracked me down by the road.'

'We've been gone longer than that, plus there's no bump on your head. They'll check you for a concussion,' Sidnee objected. She was right; they'd want him to see a doctor.

'We could say I fell into that abandoned mine, the one Connor hid in?' Danny suggested.

'No. They'll investigate, try to seal it back up and know immediately that's not true,' I replied.

'A sinkhole?'

Before I could answer that it would be the same for a sinkhole, Harry's steady voice came from the back. 'Danny was dehydrated and became disoriented. He wandered for a while, realised he was lost and hunkered down. He was planning to wait until morning to find his way out of the woods. His headlamp was dead and he didn't have his phone. The dog can still have found him.'

'Simple, and believable,' Connor said. 'Danny, do you have your phone?'

'No, I left it behind. We were supposed to be without tech.'

'What about your headlamp?'

'It must have fallen off.'

Connor nodded. 'Okay. In case someone has found it, you say it died, you discarded it and you don't know where it is.'

'Yeah, that's better,' Danny agreed.

'Perfect. Everyone got the story straight?' Everyone responded in the affirmative, including a sharp bark from Fluffy.

Connor turned left and the academy loomed up on the hill ahead. 'Here we go.' He pulled to the front and parked. The men in the back climbed out slowly and carefully as though they were exhausted, which they probably were; I knew I was close to being unconscious. Maybe I'd get better at mesmerising in the future, but for now it left me weaker than a day-old baby.

Like me, Sidnee – who'd done the most work – looked like she was hanging on by her fingernails. We were vulnerable right now, which was all the more reason for Fischer to believe the BS we were peddling.

I placed Shadow on the passenger side seat and slipped out. The poor exhausted little fella didn't stir when we shut the doors.

We gathered together and went through the front doors. Recruits and officers were scattered about the building, but someone noticed us and a shout rang out. 'You found him!' Several people pulled out phones to call their friends or fellow squad mates to tell them to come back in

'Go check on Margi,' I whispered to Sidnee before we were surrounded by a lot of relieved-looking recruits. Sidnee slipped away.

Danny was being hugged and clapped on the back. Lieutenant Fischer was glaring at our group from where he was leaning against the wall next to the reception window. He had slightly more than a five o'clock shadow and I wanted to smirk because I knew that we'd been stressing him out. He was the only one, besides whatever MIB plants there were and possibly Sergeant Marks, who knew the truth.

A table had been set up with doughnuts, coffee and hot chocolate for the searchers. They'd been going out on rotation to avoid getting too wet and cold, as well as to get some rest. We went to get a sorely needed hot drink.

Fifteen minutes later, Sergeant Marks burst through the door, took one look at us and pulled Danny into a brief man hug. 'Are you alright? What happened?' He looked sincere and I really hoped he wasn't one of *them*.

I heard Danny start to recite the story we'd come up with, but Sidnee was signalling me from the stairs and I couldn't hang around to listen. I squeezed Connor's hand, pointed at Sidnee and left him with Danny, Fluffy and the others, then I slipped behind the crowd and ran up the stairs.

It was dark upstairs and no one seemed to be around. 'Margi isn't in our room,' Sidnee said grimly. 'I checked everywhere upstairs. She's not here and neither is Eben.'

'Shit. Do we know if they made it back?' I asked.

She shook her head. 'I didn't want to draw attention to the fact that they're missing.'

'We have no choice. Let's go back downstairs and ask if anyone has seen them.'

We rejoined our group. People were fussing over Fluffy, who was accepting the admiration with a lolling tongue and a happy wagging tail. Connor was leaning against the entrance, staying out of the way. I joined him. 'Margi isn't upstairs. We're going to ask around.'

He nodded. 'I'll wait.'

We spread out, casually asking if anyone had seen Margi or Eben. Of all people, it was Thorsen who responded. 'Yeah, I saw them a couple of hours ago. Maybe they went back out to search?' He still wasn't showing any antagonism; either my mesmerising was still working or he didn't know Margi was supernat. But if Eben was working with the MIB, surely Thorsen knew the identity of all the supernats were – so that meant my mes was holding.

I grimaced at his comment. Margi and Eben hadn't gone back outside to help; Margi would have waited inside because she knew that Danny had been kidnapped, so she wasn't going to wander around aimlessly for hours. That meant that Eben had her secured somewhere, most likely on campus – and I thought I knew where. It was the one place that was more forbidden than the offices, somewhere that was locked against even the officers: the plant room under the building.

I sidled over to Sidnee and Connor. We had to distract the lieutenant so we could slip away from his watchful gaze to the basement. Occasionally a recruit grabbed Fischer's attention and they'd chat, but that wasn't enough; I needed him to be drawn away for more than a few minutes.

'We need a big distraction,' I said to Sidnee. 'A big one. Even Fluffy wouldn't be distraction this time. We need an explosion – or a fire.' I looked at my companions. 'I have an idea.'

'Let me guess. It involves fire?' Sidnee asked sarcastically.

I grinned. 'It totally does. You guys go to Fluffy and get everyone's eyes on you for a minute. I need to disappear.'

Connor and Sidnee joined the crowd that was still adoring Fluffy, and Sidnee immediately started talking about his exploits when we'd helped her back home in 'Seldovia.' Even the lieutenant wandered over, probably because he'd had his eye on Connor. He *had* to know who and what Connor was – the MIB would be familiar with the vampire king of America's son. But Connor could handle himself so I melted to the back of the throng and escaped.

I needed a place where I'd be completely alone and I found it in one of the smaller classrooms. I checked the corridor and slipped inside when no one was looking. I left the lights off.

I let my rage at the entire situation fill my body. Killing those soldiers, the kidnapping, the MIB trying to take away my rights, Eben's betrayal, my mother – the heat that simmered in my core strengthened. I stoked it until a ball of flame gathered in my chest and I focused it through my hands, then lifted them above my head and aimed for the sensors above me before I let go.

It was time to fight fire with fire.

Chapter 37

Whoops. I'd used a little too much anger. I hadn't wanted to set the whole building on fire, only to set off the fire alarm; I'd wanted a distraction, not a catastrophe.

The desk I'd aimed at flamed high and burned hot. I moved the rest of the desks away a little so it wouldn't spread easily and then I slipped out. Even as I closed the door, the fire alarm started to blare. I slipped into the toilets to wait for the building to be evacuated.

Connor and the other supernats would probably be evacuated, too, but they'd come to me as soon as they could slip away unnoticed. I headed straight to the basement – and hopefully to Margi.

I kept my eyes peeled, but I'd waited long enough and the building was empty. Sirens wailed in the distance so it wouldn't be long until the fire brigade arrived. I needed to be quick. I sprinted down the hall. All the doors had closed when the alarm had triggered, but no one was around to lock the door into the offices. I opened one and ran the short distance to the back door then looked for something to prop it open for Connor and Sidnee.

I didn't have anything but my phone so I slipped into an office and stole a bright-red stapler from the desk and stuck it between the door and the jamb, leaving about an inch and a half opening. Perfect.

Between the fire brigade's imminent arrival and the risk to Margi's life, I couldn't wait for backup. The basement door stared at me. This time, though, I cared not a whit about being discovered since this whole thing was clearly going full Armageddon. I didn't bother with a spell. I grabbed the door and ripped through the lock and tore the door off two hinges. Whoa. Vamp strength with a little adrenaline, and I was the Hulk.

Door battered open, I raced down the steps as silently as I could. If I was right and Eben was human, he probably wouldn't hear me over the noise of the fire alarm and the plant equipment – but there was always the chance he wasn't alone.

I peered down the corridor but I couldn't see anyone. What if I was wrong about where Margi was being held? What if they'd taken her to another waterfront building? Crap on a cracker.

I raced to the bottom of the steps and peered through the door. I still couldn't see anyone but I could hear Eben's voice. I'd guessed right. Fist pump.

'You witches – so powerful.' He spat out the last word sarcastically with a hefty dose of malice. 'Let's see you do magic now, huh? You can't, can you?'

I didn't hear a reply and my gut knotted in fear. Was Margi still alive? There were very few reasons – death, exhaustion or magic-cancelling cuffs – why a witch wouldn't be able to access her magic and I prayed for the latter. I needed to hear another 'good gravy' or 'holy smokes' fall from Margi's lips. She was such a golden soul that she didn't even swear. If anyone deserved to live through this, it was her.

I crouched down and eased forward, slowly.

'You have to use your hands, don't you?' Eben sneered. 'And they're bound and unavailable. Boo-hoo.' He laughed.

Hmm. I didn't have to use my hands for *my* magic and I doubted Margi did either, so what was he talking about? Margi was a water witch and the pipes around here were full of water. Why hadn't she taken him out?

I crawled on my belly under the pipes until I could see their feet. Eben was pacing, but Margi was in a chair with restraints around her feet and a used syringe on the ground. That damned somnum drug – if Eben had used that, Margi probably wasn't even conscious. So why was he talking to her? If he was in the middle of his villain's soliloquy, I was going to use his distraction to beat some sense into him.

Thorsen had said he'd seen both of them a while earlier. If he'd been telling the truth – which I wasn't certain about – and if the drug worked the same on witches as it did shifters, Margi would probably be out for at least a couple more hours. That felt like a lot of ifs.

The syringe contents were bluish, like the one used on Danny. I wanted to sigh with relief but I held it back; there was no point in announcing my presence, though Eben seemed to be talking to himself. That was supposedly the first sign of madness, though I doubted he'd love it if I pointed that out.

He continued, 'I'm so glad I don't have to pretend to be one of you anymore. I finally feel clean again. Sharing your air was making me feel sick.'

What a total wanker. He'd be damned lucky to be a real shaman. Anissa, the one I knew in Portlock, was one of the nicest people I'd met, much nicer than this prick.

I heard someone coming down the stairs behind me and something in me eased. Connor was finally on his way. Sliding back and standing up slowly and carefully so Eben wouldn't see me, I turned to watch him come down the corridor. Relief and joy filled my sluggish heart.

Only it wasn't Connor who stepped into sight. It was Lieutenant Fischer.

For once I was speechless; I had officially run out of expletives.

Chapter 38

I looked around desperately for somewhere to hide but Fischer had seen me. A dark grin filled his face. 'Expecting someone else, recruit?' he asked. His lips had a cruel twist to them. How had I ever thought he was handsome? Silver fox, my ass; silver gorilla, more like, which worked because silver gorillas were dangerous as fuck. Oh good, my expletives were back.

I swallowed. What had he done to Connor and Sidnee? 'Maybe,' I said pugnaciously. I wasn't going to admit to anything.

Eben came around the corner and stood by the lieutenant. More people were coming down the stairs and they weren't being quiet. My heart sank; nobody but Sidnee and Connor knew I was down here…

However, the people coming down the stairs were Thorsen and Miller, the other MIB agents we'd discovered.

Sergeant Marks wasn't amongst them; either they'd used him to keep Connor and Sidnee at bay or he wasn't involved. I opened my mouth to shout for help. There were other supernats in this building and although being in the basement might muffle my screams, there was a slim chance someone might hear me.

I yelled, 'Aoife!' with everything I had and got out one good holler before the lieutenant sprayed something in my face. My voice cut off and I could no longer make a sound. And Aoife didn't show.

I choked in a breath but it was difficult because my throat was partially closed. I could breathe if I stayed still but any exertion was impossible. I put my hands to my throat and glared at the lieutenant. 'What did you do to me?' I mouthed,

Fischer seemed to understand. 'That's one of our handy new drugs – it makes you silent. It doesn't last long but we're working on it and it's more effective than duct tape. I've been longing to use it on you,' he crooned. 'Damned encyclopaedic brain, spouting the answers like a little know-it-all, showing everyone else up. Well, now I have you, Elizabeth Octavia Barrington.'

He smiled smugly then motioned Thorsen to come forward and tie me up. 'I know you vamps don't need to breathe, but I'm sure this will still be uncomfortable. If you don't struggle, we'll get you out of here to our submarine soon enough. First we need to collect the others then it'll be time for you to go away and for me to greet the next bunch of recruits.'

I glared at him. Someone was going to notice if a full cohort of supernats went missing, even with the lack of communication between the various supernatural safe havens. This couldn't be swept under the rug and that thought gave me some comfort.

Fischer gestured to someone down the corridor and one of Thorsen's cabal came forward carrying Sidnee over his shoulder. Two more of them were dragging Connor. They secured their bonds and leaned them against the wall next to me. I choked back a sob as hope drained from me. A rescue team wasn't coming. *I* was the rescue team – and I was so screwed.

'Shouldn't be long, but we need to find the other three supernat recruits and that bastard Marks. Seems they received a warning.' Fischer glared at Connor's limp body. Although Connor wasn't breathing, he was a true vamp; he had to be alright or they wouldn't have brought him down here. Sidnee's breathing was slow and steady: she was out, but she was okay.

But where was Fluffy? At least Shadow was sleeping safely in the truck and no one knew about him. It was a small consolation as the rest of my life went down the pan. As if he'd read my mind, the lieutenant asked, 'Where's the vamp's mutt?'

'We tied him up like you said,' Miller answered. 'We could do with a highly trained K-9.'

The lieutenant nodded. 'Saves us some money on training.'

Were they keeping Fluffy for the State Troopers or the MIB? For his sake, I hoped it was the former. I was relieved the bastards hadn't shot him; they didn't like supernats but they understood the importance of a good dog. I hoped Fluffy would go along with the subterfuge until he could escape and get back to Gunnar. Gunnar would take care of him.

Oh man, Gunnar was going to be so mad when Sidnee and I didn't return from the academy. Fischer didn't know what kind of hell he was bringing down on his head. If I'd worked it out, so would Gunnar – and Gunnar would be prepared with backup and seventeen different types of weapon. He was a demi-god; he would make them regret their every action. Knowing that steeled my spine. Whatever happened to me, Gunnar would make them pay.

It had to be enough.

Chapter 39

I gritted my teeth. I would not give up hope and resign myself to this fate. Danny, Harry, George and Sergeant Marks were still free, and none of the enemy knew that I had fire magic. I needed to *think* my way out of this; I had time as long as I kept a level head and didn't panic.

Lieutenant Fischer was hissing angrily at Thorsen; he was trying to keep his voice down, so naturally I strained my ears to hear what he was saying. I only snatched a word or two, but it seemed like Thorsen was arguing with him. Was my earlier mesmerising still making him sympathetic to supernaturals?

Hope blossomed in my heart – then rapidly died as I heard more of their argument because they were arguing about injecting me. Thorsen was all for it but the lieutenant wasn't. They had four more people to bring in and only two more doses of somnum. Since I was already tied up, there was no need to waste another valuable dose on me. But it was good to know that I'd rattled Thorsen's cage enough for him to be afraid of me.

Predictably, the lieutenant won the discussion; this was Fischer's territory so he won the pissing contest and several of the MIB soldiers went off with the two remaining syringes to bring back the four missing supernats.

I tested the cuffs again: they were tight. The tensile strength of these suckers was more than 180 kilos. I might have been able to break them if I'd had some leverage but I had none.

The remaining MIB group ignored me, except Thorsen who sent me a couple of anxious glances. If my hands had been free, I'd totally have finger waved to get more under his skin.

I was trying to get a plan together that didn't involve setting myself on fire as well as them until I heard a squeaky little meow. My heart stopped. *Shadow?* Another wave of fear hit me and I felt nauseous. Had Fischer's men got him too, or had he slunk down here all alone to create carnage?

There were no shouts or comments about a damned cat, so the chances were good that Shadow was down here of his own volition. How the hell had he gotten out of the truck? Suddenly I realised: the back window. I'd opened it to speak to the others and I'd forgotten to close it when we'd left the truck with the lynx kitten sleeping inside the cab.

No one noticed my little guy; with his smoky fur, he merged into the shadows whose name he bore. Even so, fear juddered through me. He was my little fur baby, not a highly trained police dog or a valuable supernat. To these guys, he'd be a *varmint*, something to shoot at. Plus Shadow must have used up his strength earlier so I doubted he could defend himself with his freaky shadow powers. He'd be limited to teeth and claws, and he was still only half grown.

I couldn't signal him to tell him to go away in case the men saw me – and anyway, Shadow was a *cat* so he'd probably ignore me. I looked at my friends but they were still unconscious, and Fluffy was tied up elsewhere. There was only me, an army of one.

I needed to melt the cuffs that were binding me. I thought about my mum's comment that really powerful witches could make small flames, while mid-range fire witches could only make big ones. Well, if Mum could do it, so could I. The only problem was that I'd never learned how to do something that precise.

Shadow walked into the room and made a beeline for me. I glanced around desperately to see if anyone had noticed but he'd gone under the pipes and no one had reacted. I had to work fast.

I let the frustration and anger build the heat that lived in my centre then forced the fire down my arms. The trick was to stop it at my wrists and temper it from an inferno to a small, butane-torch level. Probably. I pictured a small, high-temperature flame in my head, so hot it was blue, and directed it at a spot on my wrist.

Heat poured out of me. Sweat ran down my face, dripped into my eyes, pooled in the small of my back. It was already warm in the basement and I'd raised the temperature of the room by several degrees more. I glanced up to see if the men had noticed. One of them was absent-mindedly wiping away a bead of sweat from his brow but none of them were looking at me. More fool them.

I concentrated: *small flame, small flame,* I thought.

I had no idea if it was working until suddenly the nylon cuffs melted and hot liquid dripped on my skin. The burn was excruciating but I muffled my gasp before it could escape. I couldn't let them have any warning before I attacked. My chances were already slim and the best I could hope for was the element of surprise.

It was time to go out swinging.

Chapter 40

My hands snapped free. Almost at the same time, Shadow strolled out from beneath the pipes and slow-blinked at me. He sat down and yawned, showing his very white, very sharp teeth, then he looked around and saw Connor, who'd been tossed like a sack against the wall.

Shadow strolled over and jumped onto his stomach. Connor stirred and Shadow laid down and started to purr. Loudly. My heart gave two hard beats. To my sharp supernat hearing, the sound was virtually roaring around the confines of the room. *Please don't let them hear*, I begged the universe.

The soldiers kept on talking and ignored us.

Connor's head slowly rotated towards me and he blinked several times in surprise. Yes! Whatever Shadow had done by jumping on him and purring had freed him from the somnum. I'd heard that cats' purrs could be healing but Shadow's must have been off the scale. Was that another power he had? Or didn't the blue drug work for long on vamps? That was something to think about later. Whatever had helped Connor, I didn't care; the universe was *totally* on our side.

Now I had to get close enough to him to burn away his bonds, but I couldn't do that without seeing what I was doing or I'd burn him instead. Regardless, Hope was wiping her nose and getting back up yet again – God, I loved her. She was the grittiest of bitches; no matter how many times she got stamped down, she kept getting back up.

My burns were itching so at least they were healing, maybe not completely until I drank some blood but enough that the pain wasn't crippling. I licked my lips and focused. If the two of us were free, we could overpower the five humans. My heart was in my throat as I inched closer to Connor, praying that the bad guys wouldn't look my way.

He locked eyes with me and I showed him that my hands were free. He nodded and rolled onto his side to give me access to his cuffs. That upset Shadow, who hopped down and batted at him with a soft paw. *Now is not the time, Shadow buddy!*

I locked my fingers around the furthest bit of cuff from Connor's skin then, keeping my flame small, melted away the restraints. Connor smiled, reached up and caressed my face, then he gazed over at the men and mouthed, 'On three.'

He held up three fingers and counted down. In a move as smooth as silk, he leapt to his feet. I was a second behind him and we rushed the group together, vamp speed. Thorsen was facing us and his eyes flew open wide. The lieutenant had the quickest reaction: he pulled out a high-tech looking gun and aimed it at Connor.

I recognised it instantly. 'Taser!' I yelled. My voice was back! A gun could kill us if it was a direct heart or head shot, and a taser shooting 1500 volts would disrupt a vamp's nervous system the same as a human's. I knew that from experience…

But it turned out that summoning Aoife had worked. She'd been biding her time but now she materialised in front of Fischer – and she *screamed*.

The human men fell like dominoes at the might of an angry banshee wail. Connor and I didn't waste a second of the time she was giving us. Even as our own ears started to bleed, we grabbed flex cuffs from the prostate men and cuffed them. Man, that was satisfying.

Blood was dripping from their ears; clearly they couldn't hear a damned thing and they were in agony. That gave me a grim sense of pleasure: they had stolen my voice so we had stolen their hearing. Tit for tat. Of course Aoife's scream had rendered my ears silent, but that was nothing a little blood wouldn't fix.

Connor had clearly had the same thought. He bit down on the other toady, who might as well have been wearing a red shirt for all his chances of survival, and drank until his ears were working again. He shoved the man at me and mouthed, 'Drink.'

Ack – I hated drinking from the source because the one time I'd done it I'd nearly lost myself. Connor shoved the man at me again and instinct made my fangs slide down. I was buried in the guy's neck before I could blink and hot blood was bubbling into my mouth, warm blood was *so* much better than the cold shit I'd been ingesting! I swallowed it until my hearing came back with a pop.

I must have paused or given some other sign I was okay because Connor pulled the toady off me and shoved him back to the floor. Mealtime was over. The urge to keep on drinking was so strong that I had to take some deep breaths. I guessed vampirism was a little like Pringles: once you popped, you couldn't stop.

'Okay?' Connor asked, concerned. I gave him a thumbs up because I knew he'd detect the lie in my voice if I said I was fine.

Thorsen had taken advantage of the momentary lapse in our concentration, stumbled to his feet and run out. In all the screaming and drinking, neither of us had remembered to secure him. I wasn't worried because I knew he wouldn't get far, but before I could chase after him, Shadow bounded off. I tried to call him back but no words came out.

We checked Margi and Sidnee; they were both unconscious but their ears weren't bleeding. 'How come Aoife's scream didn't hurt them?' I asked Connor.

'You have to be conscious for a banshee wail to work.'

There was a piercing cry from the corridor and we ran out to see what was going on. In the dim light I saw Thorsen sitting on the floor, cowering; in front of him, between him and the stairs, was a gigantic lynx. *My* gigantic lynx!

I grinned. Shadow was huge, at least ten times the size of a normal full-grown lynx, and closer to two hundred kilos than ten. He was standing menacingly, eyes glowing gold and silvery fur standing up in all directions. Even his little stub tail was a puff of fuzz. His growl was low, serious – and utterly terrifying.

I beamed. 'What a good boy,' I praised. Shadow gave a happy purr but in his current form it came out as a rumbling roar. Cool.

'Got any more flex cuffs?' Connor asked me.

I looked down at my hand, surprised I was still clutching the cuffs I'd taken from the lieutenant. 'Yeah, here.' He bound Thorsen tightly. To be honest, Thorsen looked relieved to be dragged back to the other room away from Shadow.

I looked back to see my kitten shrink back to his regular ten-kilogram self. Once he was his correct size, his shadow oozed back onto his fur. It looked like it came from inside his skin and I shuddered: *he could use his shadow to increase his size?* He was a pure supernatural anomaly, an unknown cryptid. I guessed it was up to me to unlock his secrets and his connection with the beast beyond the barrier. Whatever, he was my very best boy.

Connor and I weren't done yet: we had to stop the remaining MIB assholes from injecting my friends and somehow disable them. The lieutenant had said there was a submarine waiting, which meant there were more MIB out there. He must have had some type of communication device to signal them to send a boat or a skiff to get everyone to the sub. Our time was growing short.

'We have to search them,' I said to Connor. 'One of them – probably the lieutenant – must be able to get in touch with that sub.'

The lieutenant did indeed have a communication device – and so did the other men. We confiscated them all; with their ruined eardrums, it wasn't like they'd be using them anytime soon.

Connor and I plugged the devices into our own ears; they were already switched on and an occasional smattering of conversation came through.

'We have to leave with the tide. You have forty-five minutes. Acknowledge.'

Connor and I looked at each other, then he clicked the button to speak. 'Acknowledged.'

Nothing else came through. 'Guess it worked,' he said.

'I hope so. We need to save the others,' I said.

The adrenaline was receding now, leaving me feeling more tired than ever. My hands started to shake and suddenly everything hit me. Why were these people so angry at supernats? I was like *them*: I wanted to go to work, earn a living, enjoy my pets and my boyfriend, and live a comfortable life. I wanted to go home to Portlock and curl up with my pets and Connor and a cup of tea – a proper one not like the crap they had here. How was my vampirism hurting them? How was my best friend being a mermaid a risk to national security? The fact that we were different changed *nothing*.

It always came down to fear. Since we had a different sort of power to them, they had to take it from us and eliminate us to feel safe. And that meant we supernats had to stay hidden. Well, screw that.

Connor must have noticed me spiralling because his comforting hand at the small of my back grounded me again. We had a mission to stop this mess, save the supernats and the academy, then help the state by taking the financial papers to people who would know what to do with them.

'Take a deep breath, Bunny,' Connor said gently. 'We'll get to the others, then we'll expose these fuckers so they can't continue their little supernat disposal plan.'

'How? How do we do it while keeping our existence secret? We can't expose the whole supernatural world.'

'We won't. We'll use the law,' he said confidently.

'How?' I asked again.

He held up the syringe, clasped in a scrap of paper so he wouldn't leave fingerprints. He must have picked up the one that had been left at Margi's feet. 'Evidence.'

He was right – and I needed to pull myself together. I was an officer of the Nomo's office of Portlock; I was the law. I was also a recruit at the State Trooper Academy and I could recall every single lesson we'd had. We would bring them down as *humans*.

I straightened up. 'You're right. I just needed a moment. The Shadow-cat situation threw me for a moment, but I'm totally fine.'

My half-grown kitten rubbed against my legs and I leaned down to stroke his silky fur. 'You are a rascal. We'll figure you out some day ... but in the meantime, please stay here and stay out of trouble! Go watch over Sidnee. We'll be right back.'

For once Shadow did as I asked and he walked down the corridor to the plant room. I hesitated. I didn't want to leave Sidnee and Margi if any of those assholes were conscious.

It didn't take much to bend my morals a little, and I went back into the room and hit each man over the head so they passed out. Better. I removed Sidnee's cuffs and moved her to the anteroom so she wouldn't be with them when she woke up, then Connor and I removed Margi's restraints, lifted her off her chair and laid her down next to Sidnee.

'Okay, now we can go,' I said. We still had Eben and a couple of the other MIB to deal with, but that was doable.

We raced up the stairs and burst out the door at the top – which I closed as firmly as I could so Shadow wouldn't do anything else strange in full view of the entire academy. To my surprise, most of the staff and recruits were still milling around the main entrance. The fire seemed like a lifetime ago, but we hadn't been gone more than half an hour. Apparently, the event required a debriefing and copious amounts of doughnuts and hot cocoa; it was the academy's solution to everything, and it was hard to argue with.

I scanned the crowd. Danny, Harry and George were surrounded by other recruits, which had probably prevented them being injected and dragged down to the basement. A wave of relief weakened my knees and I stumbled. That was when I saw Eben and Sergeant Marks walking towards the cafeteria.

No one was down there. Was Sergeant Marks with Eben, or was Eben going to inject him and send him to the submarine? My money was on the latter. 'Connor, I'm going after Eben. Can you keep an eye on them?' I pointed to Harry, George and Danny.

'Yeah. Go.' I loved that he didn't doubt I could handle Eben.

It didn't take me long to catch up with him and Marks. There were just the three of us and the noise from out front had faded to a low murmur; no one would hear us.

'Let him go, Eben,' I said, my voice low and threatening.

Marks looked at me strangely. 'What's up, Barrington? I came to talk privately to Eben – I'll be back out in a minute if you need something.'

'No. Eben is an MIB plant. He has a syringe to inject you with then he's going to take you to a submarine and transport you to a black-ops site for experimentation.' It sounded a little far-fetched when I said it out loud. 'Trust me,' I added.

Eben gave an awkward laugh. 'Don't be weird, Barrington. I have a question about class.' He was trying to act as though I were batty, but even so Sergeant Marks backed away from him.

'He's already attacked Danny – Danny confirmed it,' I persisted.

Sergeant Marks froze. I could see the wheels turning in his brain and I saw the moment he accepted that I was telling the truth. The problem was that Eben saw it too and he leapt forward, the syringe in his hand aimed at Marks' neck.

The sergeant had been looking at me but he caught the motion out of the corner of his eye. Luckily he was a supernat and he was *fast*. He caught Eben's arm in a hard grip before the syringe touched him. I heard Eben's wrist snap and he screamed in agony.

After I plucked the syringe from his nerveless hand, Sergeant Marks threw him against the wall. Eben slid down, unconscious. I held out a hand to prevent Marks doing something he'd regret. 'That's probably enough. I've got it from here, Sarge.'

I took another set of flex cuffs from my back pocket and secured Eben's arms. Even though he was unconscious, he whimpered when I pulled his broken wrist behind him. I almost felt sorry for him before I remembered that he'd been lying to us for weeks, had kidnapped one of my friends and was planning to take us to be experimented on. Asshole.

I turned to Marks. 'We have to find a couple of Thorsen's allies because they're after Danny, George and Harry. The rest are tied up downstairs.'

'The rest?'

'Yes. The poltergeist pointed them out.' I took a deep breath; this next revelation would be a shocker to the sergeant. 'Lieutenant Fischer was involved.'

Marks shook his head vehemently. 'No, I don't believe it.'

'He, Thorsen and Miller are secured downstairs in the basement plant room. Margi and Sidnee were drugged and they're down there, too, sleeping it off.'

The sergeant scrubbed his hands over his face and muttered something I didn't pick up; from his expression I guessed they were some choice swear words. I blew out a breath; we weren't done yet. 'I need your help.'

Marks straightened. 'What do you need?'

'To come up with a good reason why we're about to arrest all of these people. I figured that the attempted kidnapping is a start.'

He nodded. 'Yeah, that should be enough to switch it to federal charges and take the locals out of it after they do the arrest. But the MIB are tricky – they'll either get these bastards off or make sure they never talk again.'

I hadn't thought of that possibility but it made sense: they were utterly ruthless. 'We'll need to prove the attempted kidnapping happened, right?'

'Yeah, we need evidence and witness statements. When the feds take over, we need to have our ducks in a row. We need to keep it strictly to kidnapping.'

'Maybe money? Ransom demands?'

'Maybe.'

I frowned. 'The MIB think ahead. These men will already have a line to toe if they get caught.'

'We'll get around it.' Marks ran his hand through his short hair and shook his head in disbelief. 'I thought Fischer was a proponent of supernat officers. But we have two jobs to do – first, save our people, and second, turn these scum over to the Sitka police. Let's do it.'

I grabbed Eben, whose fast heart rate told me he'd come around though he was playing possum for all he was worth. As I hauled him to his feet, he whimpered again and opened his eyes. 'Walk, asshole,' I snarled. Marks seized his other arm and we frogmarched him back to the crowd.

The recruits were scattered around the front entrance, still talking and eating. Marks took up a position near the reception window and raised his hands to get everyone's attention. Once he had it, he said, 'A kidnapping ring has been discovered here at the academy. If you see Brandon Steele or Dominic Olsen, you are hereby obliged to arrest them.'

Murmuring and head-turning ensued, but although the recruits looked around curiously they seemed confused rather than convinced. Sergeant Marks looked at me and shrugged. I guessed we'd have to arrest the men ourselves. That was fine; I didn't mind getting my hands dirty.

As I looked around, I spotted Steele and Olsen. They saw me coming and ran.

But not fast enough.

Chapter 41

Running was enough to convince the other recruits of their guilt and the men didn't take more than a dozen steps before they were piled on and cuffed.

'Great takedowns,' Marks praised with an easy grin. He put the two men against a wall – under guard – then sent more recruits to the basement to fetch the other conspirators. Soon all of them were sitting against the wall and Sergeant Marks was making the call for the Sitka police to come and get them. He collected the syringes from the men who'd been coming for Danny, Harry and George. Connor had kept the syringe he'd found near Margi so we could have it analysed when we got back home, but we handed over the ones that had been used on Danny and Sidnee.

Tension gradually eased from my shoulders, and I almost cried with relief when Sidnee and Margi walked down the corridor. I hugged them both then hugged

Sidnee again. I grinned as I noticed Margi making a beeline for George. He looked relieved to see her and swept her into his arms.

Sidnee was almost jumping up and down with excitement. 'We stopped the bad guys!' she crowed.

'Yeah, we did. But not all of them – now we have to stop the rest,' I said firmly.

She stopped bouncing and the happiness drained out of her as if a switch had been flipped. She nodded grimly. 'Damn right we do.' She had a huge stake in bringing them down; because of her ex, Chris, this was personal. She moved closer. 'I got a text from Thomas. He said that Engell is good people, but he isn't *ex*-MIB.'

'What do you mean?'

'He still works there in internal affairs.' She lowered her voice even further. 'But Thomas says we can trust him. He was probably working to bring down this whole thing from the inside. We could have been working together the whole time.'

I frowned. 'Fischer definitely told Marks that Engell was *former* MIB.'

'That's what Fischer had been told. It looks like Thorsen and Eben weren't the only ones undercover. Now we know about Fischer, I reckon him telling Marks was an asshole move designed to make Marks feel uncomfortable with a bogeyman living in the same building.'

I grimaced. 'Quite possibly. Fischer is *such* an asshole.' I blew out a breath. 'Where is Engell? Do you think we should talk to him?'

'I tried to find him but no one has seen him.'

'You think he's okay?'

Sidnee shrugged. 'I think he's like Batman and his services are no longer required here.'

She was right. Sirens were getting closer and soon the police arrived. Sergeant Marks spoke to them and then the interviews began. During mine I focused mostly on Miller and Thorsen's actions, but I did mention their cocaine habit and floated the idea that money might have been a factor in the kidnap plot. Wide-eyed, I casually mentioned that my family in England were super-rich. It was enough to plant some seeds.

Having three victims to hand as well as the raft of evidence we'd already collected – and witnesses who were in law enforcement and knew how to make a concise statement – meant that things moved quickly.

The police wanted those who had been drugged to be tested at the hospital, but we all refused. There was no need for any of us to have our supernat blood analysed outside of our own labs, and the police already had enough to go on. They soon hauled Fischer and his men away, although annoyingly none of that lot seemed overly concerned. They probably thought they'd be free by the end of the day. I hoped that Engell was out there somewhere making sure they weren't.

Exhaustion hit me like a tonne of bricks, but I had to find Fluffy and my damned cat who had definitely *not* been in the basement when Sidnee and Margi left. I wasn't really worried about Shadow; if this experience had taught me anything, it was that my freakish lynx could absolutely look after himself. And me.

I ran outside and called for Fluffy. I knew he'd been tied up somewhere nearby until I could collect him. He barked instantly and I pinpointed his location; the poor boy was tied to a tree and the grooves in the ground left by his pacing showed that he'd been trying to get away. There had been too many observers around for him to shift.

I ruffled his ears and patted him. 'Are you okay?' He gave a low whine but wagged his tail. 'I hear you. What a mess. I'm sorry – but if it is any consolation, they got us too.'

I unclipped his lead and removed it from the tree. Fluffy yipped and leaned against me gratefully as I sank down and gave him a full body cuddle, something I needed as much as he did. I buried my face into his fur and clung to him for a long minute. Eventually I gave him one last squeeze and stood up. 'Do you mind helping me find Shadow? He's had a big night and I'm afraid he's disappeared. Again.'

Fluffy whined again and looked concerned; in truth, most of the time Shadow was more his pet than mine. He took off like a shot and ran straight to Connor's truck. The first thing I noticed was the open back window that had led to trouble in the first place. 'He escaped from there and the basement, Fluffy. I don't know where he went.'

When I turned away, he barked again. 'Fine,' I huffed. I opened the door – and lying on the passenger seat where we'd left him earlier was Shadow, curled up asleep. Another layer of stress disappeared.

'You little beast.' I reached in and stroked him softly. He didn't move; he must have been completely worn out after his escapades. I leaned over to shut the back window then closed the door. No more adventures for him tonight.

I still needed to retrieve the papers – if they'd stayed hidden. The police were searching the lieutenant's office and I was sure someone was searching Fischer's home, but the documents weren't meant for human eyes and I needed to get them to the right people. Gods, I was tired.

I dragged myself and Fluffy back inside the academy. Connor was waiting and since there was so much confusion, I took them both into the break room to see if the bag was still there.

The room had been torn apart and for a moment I lost hope. My rucksack was still on the floor by the sofa; it had been opened but not emptied. The snacks on top must have been enough of a deterrent. I breathed a sigh of relief but just to make sure, I took out everything I'd used to hide the papers. They were all there! I gave a fist pump and Connor pulled me in for a congratulatory hug – which became a scorching kiss.

'Hey, no fraternising here!' Sidnee's teasing voice interrupted us.

We pulled apart with sheepish expressions. 'Soon,' I whispered.

'Yeah, soon.' He rested his forehead against mine and we breathed together for a moment then he pulled back, reluctance in every line of his body. 'This has been a clusterfuck,' he said. 'But you have to finish what you started.' He looked at Sidnee. 'Both of you. A few more weeks and your education will be officially complete. You've got to push through.'

I sighed. 'You're right, but my need for home is strong.' Really, really strong.

'Home will be waiting for you,' he murmured.

He gave me another long slow kiss and Sidnee huffed audibly. 'You guys are killing me,' she grumped.

'Sorry,' I apologised.

Her eyes softened. 'Don't apologise for being in love. I'm fifty shades of green.'

Connor grinned. 'I was going to make a joke but my brain realised it was inappropriate before my mouth got there.'

Sidnee looked at him. 'And now I want to know what it was.'

He considered for a moment before shaking his head. 'Nope. I'm taking it my grave.'

'To your coffin more like,' Sidnee snarked.

'Something like that.' He stood. 'I'll speak to you later,' he promised me. 'Keep your phone handy.'

'You bet.' After all that had happened, I wouldn't be going anywhere without a way to get help in an emergency.

'I'll take these papers to Gunnar,' he said.

'Okay. tell him he might want to share them with the Nomo at Ugiuvak.'

'Roger that.'

I slid onto my knees to give Fluffy another cuddle. 'Take care,' I murmured to him. 'I'll be waiting to see you, Reggie.' He licked my face then trotted off next to Connor. They may as well have taken my heart with them. I sighed. 'Man, I miss them.'

'They literally left two seconds ago,' Sidnee laughed.

'Yeah. I don't know about you, but I'm bone tired even though it's night time!'

She laughed. 'I'm feeling weird and wired. I think I'm still shaking off whatever they gave me. I'm tired but I have one hell of a buzz.'

I sat up. 'Should we get you to a healer or the hospital?' Did the unknown drug have side effects we knew nothing about?

She shook her head. 'You know I don't do doctors unless it's absolutely necessary. Hospitals creep me out.'

'Why? They're there to help you.'

She crossed her arms and somehow looked smaller and younger; her shoulders curved inwards so much they were almost concave. 'When my parents were killed, I spent hours in a hospital all alone. No one told me what was happening or what to do or where to go. Eventually a nurse noticed me and asked me what I was doing. I broke down and she took care of me. She was the one to tell me my mum and dad were gone, then she called social services. You know the rest.'

I did. Sidnee's parents had died when she was a teenager. Because she wasn't a child – and she was a half-blood to boot – no one would take her on. That's how she'd ended up with Gunnar and Sigrid in Portlock, Alaska's last-chance saloon for supernats.

Supposedly, no one *chose* to go to Portlock though I didn't understand why because the people there were amazing. Okay, I could have done without Stan's shitty jokes, Liv's scary demeanour and the beast beyond the barrier... but I never wanted to be anywhere else. It was home, for me and for Sidnee.

Her story broke my heart. She was a wonderful person, a true and loyal friend, and I was so angry for her. Deep down that anger had to live in her heart as well; she put on a good show, but my bestie had deep and powerful issues. Someday she'd have to deal with them. 'Okay,' I said softly. 'No hospital.'

'No hospital.'

I changed the subject; she needed a break from her thoughts. 'We saved the academy.'

'I guess we did. I wonder what that'll mean? Do you think it'll be business as usual tomorrow, what with the lieutenant and a load of recruits being arrested? Will we even have class?'

I sighed. 'I have no idea, but I'm going to bed. I'll worry about it tomorrow.'

She slipped her arm through mine and we headed towards our dorm. 'Sounds good. Let's do that.'

So that's what we did.

Chapter 42

It turned out that it was indeed business as usual. We were standing in the mat room. Sidnee and I had both passed the takedown and cuffing tests and I didn't know what the next one would be.

Sergeant Marks called, 'Morning, recruits. I'm sure some of you are dying to know what the commotion was about last night.'

The murmurs got louder as the speculation started. Marks held up a hand. 'Some of you already know that the arrests happened last night because Lieutenant Fischer and a group of students were running a kidnapping ring, finding recruits that fit a certain age group to sell into a slavery. As of an hour ago, they've been taken by the FBI and they're now under their jurisdiction. I don't have any further information at this time.' The mention of a slavery ring shut everyone up.

Sergeant Marks looked uncomfortable and tugged at his collar to loosen it. 'I've heard from the leadership of the academy and we will continue with this cohort until graduation but we'll accelerate the schedule. To that end, we'll skip graves' week and do additional tests today.'

He took a breath and moved to the wall. 'We're doing the physical fitness exam today, so spread out on the mat and make sure you have plenty of space for burpees. We'll start our warmup with those.' Everyone groaned, even me. I could exercise all day – as long as I'd had blood – but no one *loved* burpees.

The physical fitness test consisted of push-ups, sit-ups and running. Sidnee and I watched the other female human recruits to make sure we faked failure around the time they gave up. Sit-ups were examined by counting how many we could do in a minute; Sergeant Marks had arranged for the supernats to be tested last so we could ensure we fell within human parameters. Sidnee and I had no trouble passing.

After the mat room, we moved outside to complete a one-and-a-half-mile run in fifteen minutes and twelve seconds. That was easy for me; since I was a university-level runner, I could let myself go a little and even pass a few men – although I had to be careful not to outrun them *all*.

Sidnee and I lined up when it was our turn. The wind had picked up and it was starting to rain. There were loud groans; nobody loved running in cold rain.

I pulled ahead of Sidnee; not only was she shorter and not built for running but I enjoyed it while she only tolerated it. I passed the other women and kept myself in the middle of the pack of men. Naturally, Sidnee and I both passed the run under the time limit.

I was walking up the hill away from everyone else to cool down when an icy wind swirled around me. An eerie voice sent chills down my spine even though I knew whose it was. 'Petrovich,' I called. 'Is that you?'

A figure coalesced in front of me: a young man dressed in an academy uniform. 'Yes. I wanted to thank you for helping the academy and finding my murderer.' His voice was uncharacteristically clear and sharp, and I wondered why.

'Your murderer?' I blinked. I totally hadn't found any murderers.

'Fischer and I were roommates. He killed me when he found out I was a shifter.'

I let out a harsh breath. Could I get a note to the FBI to somehow link Petrovich's death to Fischer? Then I realised that the word of a poltergeist wasn't going to cut it; in terms of evidence, this was a colder-than-cold case

'I'm sorry he did that to you,' I said. 'But I'm glad you're here. I wanted to thank you for warning us about the danger. You saved us all.'

He smiled and looked pleased. 'Tell Aoife, goodbye for me.' He saluted and I hastened to return the gesture. His voice faded away on the last word and he slipped from my sight – and this world.

My hand fluttered to my throat; it felt tight and my eyes were burning. Murdered. That poor man. I hoped Liam Smith had fared better; he'd almost certainly been kidnapped by the MIB, but no one knew if he'd lived or died. Maybe Engell could help Danny find out and Smith could get closure, one way or another.

From what Sergeant Marks had told us in class, supernats hadn't been admitted to the academy until about ten years ago when space had been made for a supernat instructor – Lieutenant Fischer, of all people. He must have been working this angle since then and I wondered how many supernat recruits had been taken along the way.

Most people were ignorant of our existence and it seemed safer that way. If having a few humans in the know led to people like Lieutenant Fischer furthering his own agenda, maybe it was time for us supernats to go back in the closet. It would be best to go back to no one knowing. Cloak-and-dagger shit saved lives.

I shivered. With the ghostly wind and the knowledge that Fischer had murdered Petty, I wanted to be back with my friends so I jogged back to the building. Thankfully we were dismissed to shower and get ready for flag formation and breakfast.

As I walked to our dormitory with Sid, I said quietly, 'Petty talked to me in the woods.'

She stopped and turned to me. 'No way!'

'He told me he'd been murdered.'

Her huge eyes widened even more. 'Who murdered him?'

'Fischer,' I hissed back.

'What an asshole. And to think I looked up to him this whole time – well, until the end, obviously,' she amended.

'We all did,' I said sadly. 'Lieutenant Fischer murdered Petrovich thirty years ago. I guess he's hated supernats for a long time.'

'I wonder how many more he's killed? And then he joined forces with the MIB?' Sidnee shuddered. 'There's nothing worse than a monster with power.'

'Yeah, he...' My phone was ringing in my footlocker. 'Hold on.' I dug it out but it stopped. I was expecting Connor call since he was on his way to Homer where he would transfer to Edgy's plane to ride home. But it wasn't Connor, it was Gunnar.

A prescient chill ran down my spine and I hurriedly swiped to answer. 'What's wrong?' I demanded.

'Well, I missed you too, Bunny Rabbit.' Gunnar's voice was fake jovial but I knew the difference.

'Sorry. I know you're working flat out so you're not ringing for chit-chat.'

He sighed. 'No, I'm not ringing for chit-chat. Everything is mostly fine. Connor told me some about your troubles at the academy but that's not why I called. I spoke to Sergeant Marks and he's agreed to facilitate an early graduation. You know that VSPs only need to do the nine-week training which, as soon as you take the PT test, you've completed.'

'We took it a few minutes ago.' I gestured to Sidnee and she sat next to me on my bed. I put the phone on speaker. 'He's getting us to graduate early,' I told her, then asked, 'Gunnar, what's happening? You wouldn't pull us early if something wasn't wrong.'

Sidnee cocked her head and leaned down to the phone. 'What is it, Gunnar?' she pressed.

I pictured him scratching his beard. He did that when something unpleasant was coming. 'Couple of things,' he said. 'First, I'm not happy that you're in danger. Connor said both of you had been directly targeted.'

I frowned. 'That danger has been dealt with. We brought down a kidnapping ring.'

A familiar metal squeak in the background helped me visualise Gunnar leaning forward and putting his elbows on his desk. 'Yeah, yeah, I've no doubt you figured it all out. Truthfully, that's why I need you both home. This one is going to need some out-of-the-box thinking.'

Sidnee and I were nearly vibrating with the tension he'd been building. 'This one?' I asked. There was a beat of silence.

Sidnee couldn't take it any longer. 'Gunnar, you're hedging. Spill it, boss.'

He gave a flat laugh. 'You know me too well. There's been a death.'

A frisson of fear hit me. 'Who died?' I was trying to picture whom I could bear to lose and no one came to mind; I didn't even want Liv to die and she'd made me want to throttle her on more than one occasion.

'There's been an incident at Chrome.'

I didn't know the name and looked at Sidnee. 'The chromite mine,' she explained.

I scanned my memory. The three main industries in Portlock were fishing, lumber and mining for chromite, a crystalline mineral used in steel production among other things. 'Was there a cave-in?' That seemed the logical conclusion.

'I'll explain when you get back. The answer is – complicated.'

'Complicated how?' I demanded. Suddenly it felt good to have another mystery to look forward to, and if Gunnar's perplexed tone was to be believed it was a doozy.

'I'll tell you when you get here. I've already arranged your travel and emailed the details. See ya when you get home.' He hung up.

Something really had him worried. He'd never call us back home unless the shit was really hitting the fan. 'What do you think?' I asked Sidnee, who looked as taken aback as I felt.

'I think Gunnar is scared or feeling he's in over his head.' She licked her lips. 'Whatever happened must have been *big*.'

She'd hit the nail on the head and a shiver of apprehension ran down my spine. We were heading home for Christmas, but I couldn't help feeling that something wicked was coming our way.

Do you want to see how annoying Shadow was for poor long suffering Connor? Grab this free bonus scene here: https://BookHip.com/TGCWTFQ

Jill and I are so excited to share the next book in this series, *The Vampire and the Case of the Hellacious Hag*, which you can now pre-order.

We are also slipping in a short Holiday story coming December 2024 called *The Vampire and the Case of the Cozy Christmas*. It is an absolutely beautiful heart-warming tale, so keep your eyes peeled for that!

Other Works by Heather

The *Portlock Paranormal Detective* Series with Jilleen Dolbeare

The Vampire and the Case of her Dastardly Death - Book 0.5 (a prequel story),

The Vampire and the Case of the Wayward Werewolf – Book 1,

The Vampire and the Case of the Secretive Siren – Book 2,

The Vampire and the Case of the Baleful Banshee – Book 3,

The Vampire and the Case of the Cursed Canine – Book 4,

The Vampire and the Case of the Perilous Poltergeist – Book 5,

The Vampire and the Case of the Cozy Christmas (coming December 2024!) – Book 5.5, and

The Vampire and the Case of the Hellacious Hag – Book 6.

The Other Realm Universe:

The *Other Realm* series

Glimmer of Dragons- Book 0.5 (a prequel story),

Glimmer of The Other- Book 1,

Glimmer of Hope- Book 2,

Glimmer of Christmas – Book 2.5 (a Christmas tale),

Glimmer of Death – Book 3,

Glimmer of Deception – Book 4,

It is recommended that you read *The Other Wolf books 1 to 3* before continuing with:

Challenge of the Court– Book 5,

Betrayal of the Court– Book 6; and

Revival of the Court– Book 7.

The *Other Wolf* Series

Defender of The Pack– Book 0.5 (a prequel story),
Protection of the Pack– Book 1,
Guardians of the Pack– Book 2,
Saviour of The Pack– Book 3,
Awakening of the Pack – Book 4,
Resurgence of the Pack – Book 5; and
Ascension of the Pack – Book 6.

The *Other Witch* Series

Rune of the Witch – Book 0.5 (a prequel story),
Hex of the Witch– Book 1,
Coven of the Witch;– Book 2,
Familiar of the Witch– Book 3; and
Destiny of the Witch – Book 4.

The *Other Detective* Series – Coming 2025

Frustrated Justice – Book 0.5 (a prequel story),
Veiled Justice – Book 1,

Mystic Justice – Book 2,
Arcane Justice – Book 3; and
Savage Jutice – Book 4

About Heather

Heather is an urban fantasy writer and mum. She was born and raised near Windsor, which gave her the misguided impression that she was close to royalty in some way. She is not, though she once got a letter from Queen Elizabeth II's lady-in-waiting.

Heather went to university in Liverpool, where she took up skydiving and met her future husband. When she's not running around after her children, she's plotting her next book and daydreaming about vampires, dragons and kick-ass heroines.

Heather is a book lover who grew up reading Brian Jacques and Anne McCaffrey. She loves to travel and once spent a month in Thailand. She vows to return.

Want to learn more about Heather? Subscribe to her newsletter for behind-the-scenes scoops, free bonus material and a cheeky peek into her world. Her subscribers will always get the heads up about the best deals on her books.

Subscribe to her Newsletter at her website www.heathergharris.com/subscribe.

Too impatient to wait for Heather's next book? Join her (ever growing!) army of supportive patrons at Patreon.

Heather's Patreon

Heather has started her very own Patreon page. What is Patreon? It's a subscription service that allows you to support Heather AND read her books way before anyone else! For a small monthly fee you could be reading Heather's next book, on a weekly chapter-by-chapter basis (in its roughest draft form!) in the next week or two. If you hit "Join the community" you can follow Heather along for FREE, though you won't get access to all the good stuff, like early release books, polls, live Q&A's, character art and more! You can even have a video call with Heather or have a character named after you! Heather's current patrons are getting to read a novella called House Bound which isn't available anywhere else, not even to her newsletter subscribers!

If you're too impatient to wait until Heather's next release, then Patreon is made for you! Join Heather's patrons here.

Heather's Shop and YouTube Channel

Heather now has her very own online shop! There you can buy oodles of glorious merchandise and audiobooks directly from her. Heather's audiobooks will still be on sale elsewhere, of course, but Heather pays her audiobook narrator *and* her cover designer - she makes the entire product - and then Audible pays her 25%. OUCH. Where possible, Heather would love it if you would buy her audiobooks directly from her, and then she can keep an amazing 90% of the money instead. Which she can reinvest in more books, in every form! But Audiobooks aren't all there is in the shop. You can get hoodies, t-shirts, mugs and more! Go and check her store out at: https://shop.heathergharris.com/

And if you don't have spare money to pay for audiobooks, Heather would still love you to experience Alyse Gibb's expert rendition of the books. You can listen to Heather's audiobooks for free on her YouTube Channel: https://www.youtube.com/@HeatherGHarrisAuthor

Stay in Touch

Heather has been working hard on a bunch of cool things, including a new and shiny website which you'll love. Check it out at www.heathergharris.com.

If you want to hear about all Heather's latest releases – subscribe to her newsletter for news, fun and freebies. Subscribe at Heather's website www.heathergharris.com/subscribe.

Contact Info: www.heathergharris.com

Email: HeatherGHarrisAuthor@gmail.com

Social Media

Heather can also be found on a host of social medias:

Facebook Page

Facebook Reader Group

Goodreads

Bookbub

Instagram

If you get a chance, please do follow Heather on Amazon!

Reviews

Reviews feed Heather's soul. She'd really appreciate it if you could take a few moments to review her books on Amazon, Bookbub, or Goodreads and say hello.

Other Works by Jilleen

The *Paranormal Portlock Detective* Series with Heather G Harris

The Vampire and the Case of Her Dastardly Death: Book 0.5 (a prequel story), and

The Vampire and the Case of the Wayward Werewolf: Book 1,

The Vampire and the Case of the Secretive Siren: Book 2,

The Vampire and the Case of the Baleful Banshee: Book 3,

The Vampire and the Case of the Cursed Canine: Book 4

The Vampire and the Case of the Perilous Poltergeist: Book 5

The Vampire and the Case of the Cozy Christmas; Book 5.5, and

The Vampire and the Case of the Hellacious Hag – Book 6

The *Splintered Magic* Series:

Splintercat: Book 0.5 (a prequel story),

Splintered Magic: Book 1,

Splintered Veil: Book 2,

Splintered Fate: Book 3,

Splintered Haven: Book 4,

Splintered Secret: Book 5, and

Splintered Destiny: Book 6.

The *Splintered Realms* Series:

Borrowed Magic: Book 0.5 (a prequel story)

Borrowed Amulet: Book 1; and

Borrowed Chaos: Book 2.

The *Shadow Winged* Chronicles:

Shadow Lair: Book 0.5 (a prequel story),
Shadow Winged: Book 1,
Shadow Wolf: Book 1.5,
Shadow Strife: Book 2,
Shadow Witch: Book 2.5, and
Shadow War: Book 3.

About the Author - Jilleen

About Jilleen

Jilleen Dolbeare writes urban fantasy and paranormal women's fiction. She loves stories with strong women, adventure, and humor, with a side helping of myth and folklore.

While living in the Arctic, she learned to keep her stakes sharp for the 67 days of night. She talks to the ravens that follow her when she takes long walks with her cats in their stroller, and she's learned how to keep the wolves at bay.

Jilleen lives with her husband and two hungry cats in Alaska where she also discovered her love and admiration of the Alaska Native peoples and their folklore.

Stay in Touch

Jill can be reached through her website https://jilleendolbeareauthor.com/

Jill has also just joined Patreon! What is Patreon? It's a subscription service that allows you to support Jilleen AND read her books way before anyone else! For a small monthly fee you could be reading Jill's next book, on a weekly chapter-by-chapter basis (in its roughest draft form!) in the next week or two.

If you're too impatient to wait until Jilleen's next release, then Patreon is made for you! Join Jilleen's patrons here.

Social Media

Jill can be found on a host of social media sites so track her down here.

Review Request!

Wow! You finished the book. Go you!

Thanks for reading it. We appreciate it! Please, please, please consider leaving an honest review. Love it or hate it, authors can only sell books if they get reviews. If we don't sell books, Jill can't afford cat food. If Jill can't buy cat food, the little bastards will scavenge her sad, broken body. Then there will be no more books. Jill's kitties have sunken cheeks and swollen tummies and can't wait to eat Jill. Please help by leaving that review! (Heather has a dog, so she probably won't be eaten, but she'd really like Jill to live, so... please review).

If you're a reviewer, you have our eternal gratitude.

Printed in Great Britain
by Amazon